INTERFERENCE

INTERFERENCE

AMÉLIE ANTOINE

TRANSLATED BY MAREN BAUDET-LACKNER

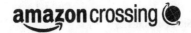

Text copyright © 2015 Amélie Antoine
Translation copyright © 2016 Maren Baudet-Lackner

Previously published as *Fidèle au poste* by Amélie Antoine in 2015 in France. Translated from French by Maren Baudet-Lackner. First published in English by AmazonCrossing in 2016.

Published by AmazonCrossing, Seattle

www.apub.com

Amazon, the Amazon logo, and AmazonCrossing are trademarks of Amazon.com, Inc., or its affiliates.

ISBN-13: 9781503936171
ISBN-10: 1503936171

Cover design by Rex Bonomelli

Printed in the United States of America

To Samuel,
who spent many hours contemplating my face while
sucking his thumb as I wrote this story.

CHAPTER 1
MAY 16, 2013

CHLOÉ

Gabriel will worry, of course. He's always worrying about me, wondering if I'm okay, hoping nothing has happened to me. He's not an anxious kind of person, though. It's just that I'm his whole world and he's terrified of losing me. He puts up an aloof exterior to hide his vulnerability, a bottomless pit of anxiety that probably wasn't there before he met me and came to care about me. I love Gabriel, and I love that he loves me. I love how he makes me feel about myself, and I love knowing that he's nothing without me.

Maybe I should be using the past tense? I'm not sure. I feel like I'm in the here and now, as if the future and the past don't exist anymore. As if this moment could go on indefinitely.

How will he feel about all this? He'll be sad, I'm sure. Devastated, even. That's understandable. Then he'll be angry. I've rarely seen Gabriel mad. He's such an accommodating person, so quick to forgive others their faults and so easy to get along with. But I know he'll be angry this time. Angry with me and with himself. He'll be mad that I let something like this happen to us. And mad that he couldn't stop it, that he couldn't *control* me and protect me from myself.

In three months, I'll be thirty. To think that he'll have to cancel the surprise party he has planned . . . I guess I should say "that he must have planned." But Gabriel is so predictable that I'm absolutely sure he's organized a celebration in my honor. Knowing him, he's probably already taken care of everything months in advance. He'll have invited all our friends, my family, and my coworkers, back in January, just to make sure everyone will be available, that no one will stand me up on the day I leave my twenties behind. He's right to plan ahead, since my birthday falls in the middle of August. He knows how often I've been disappointed in the past. In elementary school, my classmates were always on vacation when my parents wanted to schedule my birthday party. After a few years, we started inviting everyone to celebrate at the end of June, but it wasn't the same for me. In middle school and high school, I learned to have my party at the end of the school year, before everyone fled Paris for the summer. So I've rarely blown out my candles on my actual birthday.

He'll have reserved a venue and hired a caterer for the buffet and a DJ for the music. He'll have gotten everyone to go in on a group gift, something I'll absolutely love even though it never would have occurred to me to want it in the first place. Sometimes I think he knows me better than I know myself . . .

Maybe he's even planned what kind of cake he'll spend half a day making, with several layers, shiny icing, and exotic fruit decorations. Thirty candles will sit on top, rather than those lousy "3" and "0" number candles, which I would blow out in a millisecond. Thirty trick candles—the kind that relight themselves—so he can take enough pictures of me blowing them out.

Later, he'll choose the best picture of me—one where my eyes are open and I'm blowing out the candles with a happy yet concentrated look on my face—have it printed, and lovingly add it to our photo album.

Or rather, that's how it should have happened. But what good are regrets—what's done is done. I'm not the kind of person to sit around and bemoan my fate.

Right now, Gabriel is still in the shower. Soon he'll grab his towel, wrap it around his hips, and take his toothbrush out of the cup on the right side of the bathroom sink. He'll wipe away just enough steam from the mirror to catch a glimpse of his face and quickly do his hair. After stepping into a pair of crisp black pants, he'll iron a white shirt, then put it on and button it as he heads down the stairs. He'll check the time on his phone, realize he's running late, throw on his suit jacket, grab his wallet and car keys, and accidentally slam the door behind himself. He'll think about the fact that he didn't have any breakfast and console himself with the thought of the cup of coffee he'll have with his nine o'clock client when he gets to the bank.

Just like every morning.

I feel like I can predict all of Gabriel's actions, both because they hardly ever change and because after eight years of living together— three of which as a married couple—I know everything about him. Though I can hardly believe it, I almost miss all his little habits now, the same ones that used to seem so boring and even obnoxious.

I can already imagine the hurt face he'll make when he finds out. The way he'll retreat into himself, how he'll want to be left alone. I feel for him, but at the same time, life is full of challenges. I believe in Gabriel enough to be sure he'll get through what's about to happen. If there's a man on earth who can, it's him.

I vacantly twirl my wedding ring around my finger with my thumb and notice the thin line of white skin beneath the band. I love how it contrasts with the rest of my hand, which gets plenty of sun. And then I realize that from this moment forward, I'm no longer running the show.

GABRIEL

The front door slams behind him and he heads quickly toward the car. He sits down behind the wheel and turns on the radio out of habit. Late yet again. He's never been a morning person. When he was little, his mother had to shake him awake four or five times before he would deign to get out of bed for school. He would try to cover his head with his pillow to drown her out, but in the end she would always drag him out from under the covers and open the blinds all the way, so he had no choice but to get up, with his bed head and heavy eyelids.

His mother was neither gentle nor patient. She was, however, efficient and organized. In her defense, taking care of three children with a husband who was away much too often had to have been beyond exhausting. She coped by implementing military-style schedules for weekday mornings, with exact times for each person's turn in the bathroom and endless lists of chores they all had to do.

Despite all that, at thirty-one, Gabriel is almost always late for work. Well, not exactly late—he cuts it close. If he has a meeting with a client at 9:15, he gets in at 9:14. That's early in somebody's book.

So, yes, he's in a rush every morning. As soon as he turns off the beeping alarm clock on his nightstand, he falls back asleep. He always thinks he's going to let himself wake up nice and slowly. But in the end, he always falls back into a deep sleep before starting awake again at the time when he should already be out the door. He jumps out of bed, makes a mad dash for the shower, perfunctorily irons his shirt, rushes downstairs, grabs the bare minimum (car keys, wallet, phone), and leaves. And yet, he's not the least bit stressed—if he were, he'd handle things differently. He simply prefers to enjoy his bed as long as possible, even if that means he has to hurry later.

Chloé was already gone when he'd finally gotten up that morning. She had planned to go for a swim before starting her day. When she works ten to seven, she always swims early in the morning. Depending on the time of year, of course. And the tide schedule. She got into that habit when they moved to Saint-Malo three years ago, just after they got married. He knows that if it weren't for the ocean, Chloé never would have agreed to leave Paris for Brittany. Of course, they left because the bank had offered Gabriel a position he couldn't refuse, and because he'd been dying to move back to his hometown for years. He knows it was a sacrifice for her to leave her friends, find a new job as a trainer in a gym, and—most of all—give up the big, bustling city, where there's always something to do. He knows all that.

She loves swimming in the waves.

He'd tried going with her at first, but he gave up before long, especially since she prefers to go in the morning when he would rather enjoy those last minutes of sleep. Besides, he tells himself, she likes going alone; that's part of the appeal. Swimming alone, without a single person around, with nothing but the waves and the sounds of her breath. It's her quiet time before facing all her clients at the gym, waiting in orderly lines for their cardio or step classes. And he respects her need for solitude. He's always liked—and even admired—her independence. Her self-confidence. He feels like she can handle anything, with or without him. Like she's with him by choice and not out of obligation.

It's 9:02 a.m. when Gabriel arrives at the bank. His first client had called his secretary to cancel his appointment, so he has half an hour of freedom to enjoy his coffee and go through his inbox. He texts Chloé to make sure they're still meeting downtown at one o'clock for a quick lunch. They'd talked about it last night, but sometimes she's surprised with last-minute changes to her schedule when she gets to work at ten.

The morning goes by quickly. From nine thirty on, he has back-to-back appointments with clients and hardly has a minute to check the time. He loves his job. When people ask what he does for a living, Chloé always says he's a banker, but he doesn't much care for the image the term conjures up of a bald, paunchy old man sitting behind an imposing wooden desk enjoying a cigar. He refers to himself as a "financial advisor." After all, that's what he does. He advises wealthy clients on their investments, from life insurance plans to high-yield savings accounts and stocks. His clients' considerable assets afford him more room to maneuver and better options than he had with his middle-class clients in Paris. He can suggest a wide range of investments with higher yields, as long as they're willing to accept a bit of risk.

Yet Gabriel is nothing like the traders who get high on risk and are addicted to the adrenaline rush they get every time the market jumps. The thing that has always motivated him, ever since he started his job, is the chance to help his clients manage their savings by finding the investments that will earn them the most money. He likes spending his days developing relationships built on trust. His goal is also to get the people he meets—the little old lady who doesn't know a thing about numbers, the family man who's worried about the future, and the golden boy who's never had to lift a finger and thinks money falls from the sky—to like him, to trust him with their savings so that he can make the most of them. For his clients, of course.

He makes it a point of honor to explain the risks they're running and what they can hope to gain as honestly as possible. He keeps them up to date concerning changes in their accounts and never hesitates to suggest a more attractive investment. He also likes the math behind it all and the resulting predictability of his job. He likes numbers, graphs, calculations, and projections. He finds them reassuring, especially compared with human reactions, which can be so unexpected. Numbers are never irrational. They never act unpredictably—unlike the people who walk into his office.

He can still remember the old man—he was about eighty—who suddenly decided to close all his accounts because his son-in-law had told him he'd found much more profitable investments for him. Gabriel tried to reason with him, to explain that the investments he was considering, though more lucrative, were also much riskier, and to suggest that given his age, putting his savings on the line might not be the best strategy. The man refused to listen and transferred every last cent. Gabriel wasn't surprised when he learned a few months later that his former client had lost more than half his savings.

At noon, Gabriel realizes he still hasn't heard back from Chloé, despite the fact that she must have arrived at the gym two hours earlier. Between appointments, he sends another text: a simple question mark to remind her to answer him about lunch. No need for words; she'll understand. Gabriel believes in minimalism when it comes to texting.

At a quarter to one, he can't decide whether to head downtown to wait for Chloé or—since he still hasn't heard back—stay at the office and order in sushi. He dials her number. It rings several times. "You've reached Chloé. Leave me a message!" Gabriel sighs and hangs up, then changes his mind. He taps "Call" on the touch screen a second time and listens to it ring. Her message starts playing again. After the beep, he clears his throat. He hates talking to machines.

"Hey, Chloé, it's me. I guess you forgot about lunch, or maybe I misunderstood? Just wanted to let you know I'm gonna eat at the office, okay? Call me back when you get this. Talk to you later."

Gabriel is neither upset nor angry. He's used to Chloé forgetting about their little dates and not taking the time to reply to his messages. She's somewhat disorganized and scatterbrained, so he doesn't take it personally. He knows that when she finally calls him back, she'll apologize—sincerely—for the mix-up and have so many things to tell him that he'll forget all about their missed lunch. She'll say, "Oh no, I totally forgot! I'm so, so, so sorry. You forgive me, though, right?" He can almost hear the distress in her voice. There's no way he could be upset with her; Chloé's like a tornado racing across the plains at top speed, a force of nature nothing can stop. He's happy to try and keep up with her unbridled pace, her desires and whims. He's always found her energy inspiring, exciting even. She never has time to slow down, and is always saying that she doesn't know how a single lifetime will be enough to accomplish everything she wants to do. Their close friends and family think that Gabriel is finally getting her to let up, but he knows all too well that Chloé is just catching her breath and restoring her energy in the safe space created by her calm, reliable husband. They balance each other out: Chloé keeps Gabriel from getting bored, and he keeps her from burning out.

He absentmindedly orders some sushi online and steps out onto the sidewalk for some fresh air while he waits for the delivery guy. He didn't have time for breakfast this morning, and he's starting to get really hungry.

EMMA

"Could you tilt your head a bit more to the left, please? Yes, just like that, on his shoulder! Look straight ahead, not at the camera, okay?"

The young bride rests her head on her husband's shoulder and tries to look angelic—probably like a model she must have seen in some women's magazine. She actually looks kind of constipated, with a stiff smile she's trying to pass off as natural.

I don't say anything, but I'm about to implode. We've been taking these corny couples pictures for two hours now: wife looking lovingly at husband; wife innocently standing with her back against a tree while husband leans his arm against the trunk in a protective and dominating stance; husband sitting on a bench with wife lying down, her head on his lap as he gazes affectionately into her eyes; etc., etc.

Honestly, what could be more clichéd? Why do couples always insist on such sappy poses? When I try to suggest a more unique approach, they refuse. The future bride always says, "Couldn't we take some more romantic pictures?" She purrs "romantic," but I hear "corny." I suggest working with an atypical setting, like a café or a train station, but the groom steers us back to the ramparts and parks "for a natural touch." I bring up funny poses and they say, "No, that doesn't really suit our personality . . ."

And this despite the fact that I only put pictures I'm at least a little proud of up on my website. The photos you don't see everywhere— unique, unusual shots. Guests running after the groom as he flees the scene. The couple in their wedding-day finest doing their grocery shopping, hailing a cab, taking the metro, or riding a Ferris wheel or roller coaster. The father of the bride's sweaty palms and rapid breathing as he walks his daughter to the altar. The best man and maid of honor practicing their speeches in a corner. Guests touching up their makeup in the restroom during the reception.

But none of that works. When people call to hire me, they inevitably check to make sure I also take "more, um, traditional pictures." Then they soften the blow: "Your work is beautiful, but we're looking for something classic . . ."

To sum things up, taking wedding pictures drives me nuts. Sure, it pays the bills, but sometimes I think that being a cleaning lady would be less monotonous. They all want the same pictures. They don't even know the word "creativity." For them, I'm not an artist; I'm a walking photo booth.

To think that the season has just started and that I'll be doing this till the end of September at least. All my Saturdays have been reserved for months. I know I shouldn't complain. It pays pretty well and doesn't require a lot of deep thought. Plus, I'm so used to shooting the same pictures over and over that it doesn't take me long to touch them up. But, man, does it bug me . . . I have nothing but disdain for all the honeys, sweethearts, babies, my loves, sweetie pies, baby dolls, sugars, pumpkins, lambs, sweet peas, Prince Charmings, and princesses. I just can't take any more "I do's," first dances, and flower-covered layer cakes. It's almost enough to put me off love altogether.

And weddings are only the tip of the iceberg. They also hire me to put together hilarious albums of the bachelor and bachelorette parties: the bride surrounded by her closest friends; the groom downing his umpteenth drink; and a host of other moments that just *have* to be preserved for posterity. Then there are the birth announcements, family portraits, baptisms, and the list goes on. They all put on cheerful smiles and show off their flawless happiness—or the appearance thereof. In fact they're all on edge because they absolutely need me to get good pictures that look spontaneous while they're really anything but, photos that seem to capture an authentic moment of happiness when it actually took a whole lot of organization and at least twenty shots to get a single frame where everyone's eyes are open.

I love photography. But not like this. Not cookie-cutter, assembly-line photography where nothing changes but the faces. What I really want is to be a photojournalist. To go on adventures, far from here, and immortalize world events. To witness moments that will go down in history: wars, armed conflicts, protests, disasters—both natural and man-made. I want to take pictures of kids playing on battlefields, of wives grieving for their husbands, of soldiers still eager to fight. I want to capture all that emotion in their facial expressions. I want people to hear the cries when they look at my photos, to be able to imagine the laughter and sobs. I want the people who see my photos to suffer alongside the man on his knees screaming at the sight of his home razed to the ground and family slaughtered, to be moved by the mother nursing her baby as the bombs fall, to be revolted by the little girl holding a doll in one hand and a gun in the other.

That's my dream. I've had a camera swung over my shoulder constantly since I was seven, when my grandfather gave me my very first one and told me it'd make me rich—not with money, but with memories. I started taking pictures of my family, trying to capture those private moments you don't see in the traditional photos organized into chronological albums sitting in closets. My parents must have felt like they were living with a paparazzo, but no matter how hard they tried to keep me from taking pictures of everything I saw, it just fueled my passion.

I have photos of them that they've never seen. Midargument, my mother yelling with her hands raised in exasperation—"It's always the same story with you!"—my father sighing and frowning, waiting for the storm to pass. My mother smoking a cigarette in her nightgown, alone in the yard, her gaze lost in the distance. My father straining fettucine in a colander, sending the noodles up into the air with a smile, showing off his talents for my benefit. My little brother, Nathan, having a temper tantrum because we never let him win at Clue: tears of rage on his cheeks, eyes closed, lips pursed tight, hands in fists. "It's not fair!" All those moments are worth so much more to me than the traditional family portrait in front of a Christmas tree or birthday cake. Moments like that prove—in a fraction of a second—that family isn't about the bland happiness we try so hard to make others believe we've achieved. These moments capture emotions, real emotions: sadness, anger, happiness, surprise . . .

Ever since I got my first camera, I've felt like I'm always looking at the world through a lens. I'm always looking for the perfect frame, the right light, and ideal colors. I develop every picture I take in black and white because I like the contrast, the dichotomy, and the way it enhances emotions.

These photos are all on my website, under the "Everyday Life" tab. When I'm not working, I traipse through the streets like Henri Cartier-Bresson, looking for a kiss, a slap, an exclamation, an outstretched hand, a sad, pleading glance, or a fit of laughter to catch on film. A child refusing to hold his father's hand, a circle of teenage girls whispering in front of their high school, a penniless man on the bus begging the ticket checker not to fine him, a waiter spilling coffee on a horrified patron. Click, click. I never stop.

So until a press agency gives me my first big break, or I manage to save up enough money and contacts to travel the world for several months, I have to put up with Mr. and Mrs. Happy. I've been scrimping and saving for two years. I've sent résumés and cover letters everywhere I can think of. Now I'm just waiting for my time to come.

I'm giving it a few more months before I leave on my own. For Syria, Iraq, Sudan, or Mali; there are plenty of choices. Nobody believes I'll actually go, but what does that matter. My father thinks I'm too dependent on the comforts of Western living to take off, and that photography isn't a career anyway. My mother thinks my plan is completely insane. I'm pretty sure she prays every night for me not to go through with it, because she's so afraid of me risking my life for a few authentic shots.

If I had more money, I would've packed my bags a long time ago. I would have treated myself to the freedom that comes with working as a freelancer, selling my photos to the highest bidder, without a single financial hiccup to interrupt my travels. I want to witness history as it happens, and share these immensely important moments with the world.

In the end, people always get what's coming to them, and soon—very soon—I'll be able to make my dreams come true. I know it. I'll do anything to make it happen.

"Could you take your wife's face in your hands and kiss her tenderly on the forehead, with your eyes closed? A little more to the left . . . There, that's perfect."

CHAPTER 2
MAY 16, 2013, 7:30 P.M.

CHLOÉ

The minutes and hours drag on as I wait. Knowing exactly what's going to happen doesn't change anything: I'm still incredibly anxious about how the day will end. I can't wait for everything to come to light, for Gabriel to finally know. But I'm scared too. I wish I could postpone the revelation, keep him from finding out for a while longer. I almost wish I could go back in time, jump up and yell, "I quit!"

It's seven thirty now. Gabriel must be worried sick. We usually text, e-mail, or call each other several times a day. We don't do cutesy love notes, but we always have little things to say, plans to confirm, grocery lists to finalize, and ideas of what to do later to share.

Last night we even talked about having lunch together in town. So he must have been waiting to hear from me since noon. He's probably sent five or six texts with more and more question marks and exclamation points, and left two or three messages on my voice mail. Maybe he even tried to reach me directly at the gym, where Elise, the receptionist, will have told him that nobody has seen me all day and that my classes had to be canceled at the last minute because no other trainers were available to sub at the drop of a hat. I can imagine Elise's angry sighs and condescending tone, which betray the jealousy she's felt toward me for years now. "Can you believe it? We had to tell clients that they'd come in for nothing, that their step class was canceled, without any sort of justified explanation! I mean, really, it's so unprofessional . . . Well, I say that now, but maybe Chloé does have a valid excuse . . . Oh really, you haven't heard from her either?"

It'll teach that bitch a lesson when she finds out what's really going on. She'll be sorry she didn't think before speaking, sorry she indulged in so much unwarranted criticism. At least there's that. I've never been able to stand her. She's been snobby with me ever since she was hired, even though I'd already been working at the gym for a year! I understand that it must not be easy to be a receptionist in a gym where all the trainers have perfect bodies. Especially for a heavy girl. With greasy hair. But that's no excuse for her contempt and cheap jabs, like her habit of changing my schedule at the last minute, for example.

Of the four trainers, I'm the only woman. And I'm not stupid: I know they hired me primarily because I'm pretty and upbeat with an amazing figure. I'm not bragging, that's just the way it is. Anyway, the same is true for the other trainers too. They're all attractive and well built. Pablo, Sébastien, and Mehdi. Three young men with tanned skin and bulging biceps under tight T-shirts. Hey, you have to motivate the clients to buy memberships somehow.

Male clients at the gym often openly hit on me, while the women wish they had my toned legs and flat stomach. I teach class after class of step aerobics, BodyCombat, BodyAttack, and Pilates. I also work individually with clients to develop training programs specifically suited to their goals: a new mom looking to drop the baby weight; a forty-something woman who's decided to firm up her glutes; a college student hoping to wow girls on the beach; an overworked executive on his way up the corporate ladder who needs to blow off steam; etc. I feel their muscles, take their measurements, and weigh them, then come up with a training plan with weekly goals. I aim for efficiency and quick results, and my clients appreciate my enthusiasm and iron will. And, of course, my body helps too.

I'm going to miss my job. I'm addicted to exercise, and I have no idea how I'm going to unwind without swimming, running, jumping, or pedaling. I know, it's stupid to think about that when it's so trivial compared to all the rest.

And I guess this whole situation won't even be hardest on me.

Eight o'clock. Will this day never end? What can I do besides wait for the other shoe to drop? What will happen to me afterward? Will I fade away? Disappear? Wait for the end?

I can see everything, but can do nothing. I'm invisible. I don't exist. And that's not something I'm used to.

Gabriel is waiting. I watch him, powerless. He's just gotten home.

"Chloé?" he calls from the foot of the stairs in a worried yet hopeful tone.

I want to answer him. At this exact moment, I want him to hear me. "I'm here," I whisper, but silence continues to reign in our home. I repeat myself, louder, "I'm here!"—but Gabriel doesn't react. My voice resonates through empty space, disembodied. I reach out my hand to touch his face, but he doesn't feel it, of course. He goes upstairs into our room, where nothing has changed since this morning. He sits down on the bed, distraught. He gets out his Nokia and redials the same number he's been calling all day. He waits. "You've reached . . ." He hangs up and throws his phone across the room. The black back pops off as it hits the wall. He runs his hand over his face, takes a deep breath, and goes to pick up the pieces. He puts it all back together and leaves the room with a defeated look on his face.

For a few minutes, I can still see the shallow crater where he sat on the bed.

GABRIEL

At eight o'clock, when Gabriel comes home from work to an empty house, he finally realizes that something is not right. Until then, he'd been successfully brushing aside the worry that had been nagging at him all day. But now a wave of anxiety floods his brain, and he does nothing to stop it.

There's nothing surprising about Chloé forgetting their lunch. Just like there's nothing surprising about her not answering her phone or calling him back from work. None of that is anything to be worried about. Most of the time she puts her phone in her gym locker and only has time to take a quick look at it between classes. While they do communicate a lot during the day, it's mostly by text or voice mail. Or by e-mail, when she's working odd hours and happens to be at home while he's at the bank.

But her not meeting him at the bank at seven thirty for a ride home when they are supposed to have dinner at his parents' house at eight thirty—*that* is not normal. The fact that she's not at home now choosing her dress is even stranger. And the fact that he still can't reach her on her cell, that she hasn't called back despite his increasingly anxious messages, definitely means something has happened to her. Though Chloé often makes fun of Gabriel's overprotectiveness, she's careful to reassure him regularly to keep him from worrying about nothing. She should have called him back by now, rolling her eyes as she said, "Why do you always imagine the worst? I didn't realize my phone was muted, that's all! And Elise set me up with another great schedule: nothing but tiny breaks, so I barely had time to shower between classes, much less text! I'll see you later, okay?"

Sitting on the bed he shares with Chloé, he listens as her voice mail picks up yet again, then throws his phone against the wall in anger. He immediately regrets it when he sees the small mark the phone has left on the taupe wall Chloé repainted just a few months ago. He makes a mental note to use some of the leftover paint in the garage to fix it before she notices.

He picks up his phone and heads back downstairs to the living room. He dials the gym, but it's after eight and nobody answers. He should have called earlier, started worrying sooner. Could she have gone out for a drink with her coworkers? No, she knew about the dinner they'd planned for tonight; they talked about it before going to bed last night, and she reminded him to buy his mother flowers or a potted plant. When he went up to their room, he even saw her pale yellow dress hanging from the closet door.

At eight thirty, he decides to go to the cove. Maybe Chloé decided to go swimming tonight instead of this morning? Maybe he misunderstood, maybe the dinner with his parents is tomorrow night, maybe . . . Gabriel's thoughts are racing, irrational and incoherent. His anxiety is overwhelming and he can't think straight anymore.

Chloé will be at the cove. He's sure of it. When he gets there, she'll be drying off with her big turquoise hibiscus-print beach towel, a surprised look on her face. "What are you doing here? Are you all right, sweetheart? You don't look so good." She'll take him in her arms but won't understand why he seems so relieved.

She has to be at the cove. If there's any place in the world he'll find her, it's there, the peaceful place they found together after moving to Saint-Malo, during one of their long walks. That day, they had parked along a quiet road outside the city and started walking as they discussed all the work that needed to be done on the house. Chloé had noticed an incredibly narrow trail that seemed to lead down to the ocean and insisted that they explore it. Gabriel had tried to get out of traipsing through the scrub and stinging nettles, but he knew that there was no point in disagreeing with his wife: when she got an idea in her head, you either followed her or watched her walk away. After a ten-minute descent resulting in ripped pants from coming too close to vengeful brambles, they'd found themselves in a tiny enclosed space: a beach that was barely fifty square feet, with the water almost licking their toes. They had sat down and watched the waves come and go with relaxing regularity. Chloé had turned toward him and whispered in a mischievous voice, "You see, it was worth ruining your pants!" As he'd wrapped his arms around her shoulders, she had leaned her head on his chest. "I wish we could stay here forever," she'd murmured. He'd nodded without speaking, simply enjoying a moment of perfect, unadulterated happiness.

Ever since that day they've kept coming back to their hidden spot to enjoy its calm, quiet solitude. Chloé comes to the cove to swim in the ocean, leaving her towel and the rest of her things on a rock near the water without having to worry about someone taking off with them while she does her laps. It's their special place.

Gabriel grabs his car keys from the table in the entryway and is about to head out the door when his phone rings. Unknown number. *Chloé?*

His heart is racing as he picks up the phone.

EMMA

I try bouncing up and down on my suitcase to zip the damn thing up. I can almost hear my mother shouting, "Be careful, Emma. There's no point in forcing it; you've put too much in it. You'll have to take some things out if you want to be able to close it!" I smile as I push as hard as I can on the lid. Done at last. Then I notice the tripod for my DSLR sitting in the middle of my living room floor, when it should be at the bottom of my red suitcase. The suitcase I must have lost at least five pounds closing!

I sigh.

Oh well, I'll put the tripod in a second bag. That way I'll have room to bring all sorts of other indispensable things I haven't thought of yet.

Tomorrow I'm leaving for Saint-Malo, where I've taken out a short-term lease on a studio apartment. In addition to my weekend bookings for weddings and baptisms, I've been hired by the tourism office to redo its entire website with recent photos of the city and its surroundings. I'm also planning to offer my services to the summer music and theater festivals that take place in the area, to build up my own website.

This summer will be a decisive time for me. In just over six months, my future will be set. Will I have enough money to go abroad and live my dream, to finally leave everything behind and dare to do what I've always wanted to do? Or will I stay here taking wedding pictures to eke out a living, and become so bitter and cynical that I scare everyone away? I've given myself six months to find out.

I think about calling my mom before getting into bed with a book, but think better of it in the end. I need some encouragement, and I'm afraid she'll tell me yet again that she doesn't understand why I need to exile myself to Brittany for months, that it certainly won't help launch my career or boost my finances, that it would be better for me to start thinking about meeting a nice guy, that she'd like to have grandchildren in a few years, that she even asked my father not to take down the swing set in the backyard just in case, etc., etc. My mother is really good at making up a whole life for me, a future that has nothing to do with what I want or with my goals.

She doesn't understand that if I don't get to live my dream, if I give up on it before I can even try, I won't have any reason to get out of bed in the morning. I can't work in an office all day like her, doing the same repetitive, insignificant tasks over and over again, going to pointless meetings. I can't handle living such a boring, routine life simply to pay the bills. That's not me. I can deal with taking phony pictures awhile longer, but only because I know it's temporary.

I sigh again as I set my tripod down on my suitcase. I promised myself I would do everything I could to make it one day. I'm not a photographer; I'm an artist. Nothing can stop me. Not my father, not my mother, and certainly not some "nice guy."

I think it'd be better to take a warm, relaxing bath. It'll be soothing after spending the whole day packing up my things. Plus, it's probably the last one I'll get for a while, since in my new place there's no tub, only a shower.

I'll get on the road early tomorrow, even though the trip will only take a few hours. I have an appointment in the afternoon with the communications manager at the tourism office so she can explain the project details, specifically the number and type of photos they need. I've got a busy week ahead.

CHAPTER 3
MAY 16, 2013, 8:30 P.M.

CHLOÉ

When I see the metal table and the body covered with a white sheet, I can't help but shiver. Even though I know it's me underneath, I feel like I'm watching a bad crime show, the kind they run in back-to-back marathons on weekday afternoons.

Seeing it all from the outside feels really strange. I'm a spectator looking down at my own lifeless body. My *dead* body, just to get it out in the open.

I'm surrounded by a silence so thick I can hardly stand it.

Gabriel receives a call at 8:34 p.m. When he hears the phone ring, he must instantly think it's me calling him back. At last, after all these hours of worrying! Maybe he'll even yell, hurling criticism born of a mix of anxiety and relief before he even hears my voice.

But it's not me on the line.

It's a police officer, or a hospital employee. It doesn't really matter.

There's no point in beating around the bush: someone tells him that they've found his wife, that they're so sorry to be the bearer of such bad news, but she'd already been dead for several hours when an unlucky fisherman brought her up with his net.

The poor man knew something was amiss when he started hoisting the netting up from the depths. More pull than usual. He even decided it was safer to stop the electric motor and pull it up by hand. He had already ripped a net the week before and couldn't afford to buy another one, especially since his winch motor was starting to go downhill as well.

He struggled for several minutes, his chest heaving, before setting eyes on his catch. It wasn't a fish. It was a body, the body of a young woman in a black one-piece bathing suit. He was so surprised by the gruesome discovery that he almost dropped everything back into the ocean. But in the end, he managed to pull Chloé up, gracelessly yanking her over the side of the boat. He laid her down on the deck and put his ear to her mouth, then tried to take her pulse. There were obviously no vital signs. Just to be sure, he tried mouth-to-mouth and cardiac massage as best he remembered from the first-aid training he'd taken at the Red Cross years earlier. Nothing. He dialed for an ambulance as he turned on the motor and sped back to shore. Somehow he found the words to describe her silent, motionless body, pale skin, and purple lips.

By the time he reached port, the ambulance was already there, lights flashing, along with a police cruiser. As the EMTs neared the small fishing boat, they exchanged a knowing glance. They took Chloé away quickly as the fisherman looked on in dismay. They placed her in a black body bag on a gurney, and the driver turned off the sirens and flashing lights. Silence engulfed the pier. The fisherman took the navy-blue beanie from his head and wrung it in his hands, muttering, "Oh my . . . Oh my . . ." over and over again.

One of the EMTs patted his shoulder in gentle commiseration and told him that he had done what needed to be done, that he couldn't have saved her, that she had been dead for quite some time before he had dragged her aboard. The fisherman nodded, relieved, and his feelings of guilt began to lift.

The ambulance left silently, with my dead body in the back.

Nowhere to go but the morgue.

Gabriel drops his phone, and the black back pops off again as it hits the tile floor in the entryway. He leans against the wall and slides to the floor until his knees are pressed to his chest. He stares blankly ahead, like a rabbit caught in the headlights of an oncoming car.

I want to scream. I want to close my eyes and not see. I don't want to see the indescribable suffering I can read in his unmoving eyes. I want to shake him, take him in my arms, tell him everything will be okay, that soon this terrible thing will be behind him, behind us. I can see him, but can't touch him. I can hear him, but can't talk to him.

"Come on, Gabriel," I mumble, but not a sound disturbs the chilling silence that has just engulfed our home.

After a few minutes, my husband gets up, a haggard look on his face. He undoes the top button of his dress shirt to breathe a bit easier and runs his hand through his hair. He slowly heads toward the stairs and drags himself up the steps. He walks down the hallway to the bathroom, and I can hear him rifling through the cabinet where I keep all my meticulously organized beauty products. My moisturizing day cream, roll-on eye cream, powder foundation, charcoal-gray eyeshadow, black eyeliner, and evening toner. Dozens of hair ties for my usual ponytail—it's the easiest thing given all my exercising.

He comes out with my hairbrush and steadies himself on the railing. He looks like he's about to faint; he's gripping the banister so tightly that his knuckles are white. He takes a deep breath, goes back down to the entryway, picks up the pieces of his phone for the second time tonight, makes sure his car keys are in his pants pocket, and steps out the front door into the dwindling daylight.

The door closes without a sound. I'm alone.

GABRIEL

Gabriel arrives outside the morgue at nine thirty. He took his time on the drive over; there was no reason to hurry. No one to save.

He parks in the small lot, turns off the ignition, and sits there, waiting. He wants to go in, take care of all of the required formalities he knows next to nothing about, and then exclaim, "That's not my wife!" when the coroner lifts the sheet off the dead body. But he also wants to run, floor the gas until he's far, far away and the whole evening seems like nothing more than a far-fetched bad dream.

In the end, a police officer opens the door to the morgue and makes his way toward Gabriel's car. He's young—hardly more than twenty-two or twenty-three years old—and clearly uncomfortable. He would undoubtedly have preferred to be on traffic duty; promotions aren't all they're cracked up to be. Usually by this time, he would be comfortably seated on the couch in his little studio apartment, drinking and watching rugby with his buddies. Unfortunately for him, the evening is far from over. When Gabriel leaves—and he hasn't even come into the morgue yet—he'll still have to write the administrative report so his boss can read it first thing tomorrow morning.

Gabriel makes it easier for the young cop by getting out of his car. He walks toward him, a bereft look on his face.

"Hello. I'm, uh . . . I'm Gabriel Hamon. I got a call earlier. About, uh . . . my wife. Chloé Hamon."

"Yes, of course. The coroner is waiting for you. I'll take you down," mumbles the officer.

He should try to prepare Gabriel for what's about to happen inside, for the blunt questions the coroner will ask. But it's all new for him too, and he's unsure of himself. It's the first time he's ever worked a real case, and to be honest, he's really still a trainee . . . So he keeps quiet and simply leads Gabriel along the morgue's dim hallways and down some stairs. When they reach the basement level, he steps aside and gestures toward the room where the coroner is waiting, inviting Gabriel to go in first.

The coroner glances up as Gabriel hesitantly enters the room. He quickly prattles off his usual speech for the circumstances, which are hardly exceptional for him. Only the faces change. The end result is always the same. He's been doing this job for more than thirty years now, so he's had more than a few bodies on his autopsy table. He's detached from it all, and meeting the family—often unavoidable— is just something he has to get through. He doesn't know how to be empathetic; he's never known how, and he's not going to learn now. Especially given all he's seen over the years.

Gabriel is there to identify the body, but when the coroner sees the anguish in his eyes, he adopts a gentler tone and shares what he knows. They brought him the body in the early afternoon. Given the degree of rigor mortis—the lower body wasn't stiff yet—he estimates she hasn't been dead long. No more than three to twelve hours.

The paunchy man clears his throat and pauses for a few seconds. He reminds himself that this isn't the kind of thing loved ones want to hear.

He continues. She must have died around nine or ten in the morning. Maybe a bit earlier. The body is in good condition, so it must not have spent more than a few hours in the water. It's lucky the fisherman happened to pull her up, because many drowning victims are never found, and if they are, it can be weeks or even months before they turn up.

The coroner hasn't performed the autopsy yet, but he's almost certain the cause of death is drowning. The first step is to identify the young woman. And that has been rather complicated, since she obviously didn't have her ID or any personal effects on her, and she hadn't been declared missing yet. The police managed to get ahold of Gabriel thanks to the bracelet the victim was wearing. A first name was engraved on the front: *Chloé*. And a date on the back: *16/8/1983*. From there, it didn't take them long to find a young woman named Chloé Hamon, maiden name Vasseur, who'd been living in Saint-Malo for the past three years.

Gabriel feels unsteady. The bracelet means there is no room for doubt; it can't be a mistake. The coroner shows him the narrow white-gold plaque and chain in a clear plastic bag. It's Chloé's. The one she has worn on her left wrist since he's known her. Gabriel gently strokes her name, engraved in italics, through the sealed evidence bag.

"Since we have the bracelet, you could choose to just ID that and give us something for a DNA match . . . I really don't have to lift up this sheet. We have enough proof. Did you remember to bring your wife's toothbrush or an article of clothing?"

Gabriel takes Chloé's hairbrush out of the plastic bag he's been fiddling with since he entered the morgue and hands it to the coroner.

The coroner thanks him with a nod. "I'll call you as soon as the results are in, all right?" He heads toward the door, letting Gabriel know he can go home.

"I want to see her."

Gabriel's voice wavers, but it's loud enough to make the coroner jump. He turns around, surprised. Usually people are relieved not to have to look at the lifeless body of someone they loved.

"Are you sure?"

Gabriel nods. Until he sees Chloé with his own eyes, he won't be able to convince himself she's not coming back. He'll always harbor that absurd hope.

The coroner sighs and walks over to the metal table. He looks at Gabriel one last time and imperceptibly shakes his head. Taking the edge of the sheet in his hands, he lowers it just enough to expose the victim's head.

Gabriel is stoic when he sees her bluish face and purple lips.

"It's her. It's my wife," he mumbles before quickly turning away. The coroner pulls the sheet back up and tries to look sad.

Without a word, Gabriel leaves the room and its harsh neon lights behind, climbs the stairs to the first floor, and pushes through the front door. Outside he takes a deep breath of fresh air.

Saint-Malo is swathed in darkness.

EMMA

My fingers are all wrinkled when I finally get out of the hot bath. I open the bathroom window to clear the steam from the mirror. I dry off quickly, wrap a towel around my chest, and study my reflection. I use my index finger to rub away the last traces of the green clay masque I put on rather sloppily in the bath and rinsed off thirty minutes later, without bothering to look in the mirror. My skin feels tight.

I examine my face. My skin is ivory. I don't even try to tan in the summer anymore—it's a waste of time. I gave it my all as a teenager, though, coating myself in monoi oil and all sorts of other tanning aids. My nose is a bit too straight; it makes my profile look funny. I always try to pose head-on or turn slightly off-center for photos. My lips are thin and I don't do much for them—I hate lipstick. My short auburn hair is exactly the shade that's in style right now. I got a pixie cut the same day I saw Emma Watson without that disheveled mane she has in *Harry Potter*. It makes me look a bit androgynous, but the effect is balanced by the way I dress and my feminine figure: my chest is on the smaller side, but my hips are generous.

Then there are my big blue eyes, my "main asset," as the beauty advisor at Sephora once explained. "You absolutely *have* to play them up!" The eyeshadows, mascara, and eyeliner she recommended are in the very back of my drawer, still in their plastic packaging. I wanted to make her happy; she really seemed to believe in her pitch. As if I had the time to put on makeup. Or even knew how!

I know how to camouflage imperfections: blemishes, blackheads, and dark circles. I know how to make eyes pop, enhance the natural colors of the iris. I can whiten teeth, eliminate fine lines, erase gray hairs . . . and deliver perfect portraits that blur the line between the real and the imaginary. But applying eyeshadow and eyeliner on an actual eyelid is not my thing.

I'm into the new "nude makeup" trend. Without the makeup.

I open the refrigerator, then close it again. It's depressingly empty, of course. I settle on a half-eaten bag of cookies and turn on the kettle to make some green tea. Before I close my computer and put it in its black bag, I check my e-mail one last time. I have a message from a certain Edith Adelstein. I click it open.

Dear Ms. Lenglet,

First off, I'd like to thank you for taking the time to contact us via our website. As the coordinator for the Brittany branch of Coping with Bereavement, I've given a great deal of thought to your offer to volunteer and am quite interested in your idea. I think it could be very helpful for the people who are trying to manage their grief by attending our group sessions.

Your idea of working with each of the participants to create a photo album that celebrates their relationship with the deceased really touched me. I think it would be an ideal exercise both in and outside of our group sessions, a chance to create something concrete as they go through the grieving process—a kind of memorial album.

For it to work, you'll need to attend our group sessions, where you'll begin to understand the participants' expectations. From there you should be able to figure out how best to use your skills to help them make it through their loss through photography.

Please feel free to contact me as soon as you are settled in Saint-Malo and are available to meet.

Best regards,
Edith Adelstein

I contacted this association just a week ago and didn't think I'd get such an enthusiastic reply so quickly. Volunteers must be rare these days. I flag the message as a reminder to reply once I get to Saint-Malo. I plan to meet with her as soon as possible and find a way to help as best I can.

I've never lost someone myself, but if photography has taught me anything, it's that memories are important. And if I can use the passion and the talent I think I have to help people in need get through a difficult time, I have every intention of doing so.

I'm preoccupied as I get ready for bed. The big move is in just a few hours. It's dark outside. My mind always starts racing at night, the cogs in my brain turning relentlessly. Is leaving a good idea? What if I regret it? Isn't it a lost cause? Do I really have a chance?

I fluff my pillow.

© *Emma Lenglet/AFP*

Someday this credit will be on the front page of newspapers worldwide.

CHAPTER 4
MAY 21, 2013

CHLOÉ

Not just anyone can attend their own funeral. Watch as their casket disappears into the grave and tears stream down distraught faces. Listen to their loved ones read speeches they have written in trembling voices.

Some of them seem less upset than I would have imagined. My older sister, Oriane, has come from Rennes with her husband; she must have left her three kids with her mother-in-law. Actually, I'm losing all sense of time, but I think today is Tuesday, so they must be at school. And the baby must be with the nanny. Glad to know I haven't disturbed her busy schedule.

My sister is wearing a black dress with a charcoal-gray jacket; she's always cold. She's not crying. I've been studying her face and haven't seen a single tear—not even dried—on her cheek. Her eyelids aren't even swollen. I can't hear any discreet sniffling and don't see a tissue clutched in her hand. I guess she's just trying to keep her sadness to herself, to maintain her dignity.

Or maybe she's not sad. It's hard to tell. I've never been able to read her. I've always felt like my own sister is a stranger. We don't look alike at all, and our personalities are total opposites. She's only two years older, but she's so old-fashioned that it feels like we're separated by a fifteen-year gap. She has everything she's ever wanted: a faithful husband who obeys her every command without any objection; three beautiful and well-behaved children who don't even know the word "no"; an ordinary job in an ordinary office with ordinary coworkers; and a house in the countryside with a big yard because "it's important for kids to be able to play outside." The only thing she's missing is a yellow Lab.

I don't even think we were close as children. She always worked hard to color in the lines while I was out having fun, climbing trees and scraping my knees without noticing. In high school, she wrote essays on Saturdays while I went to parties and discovered tequila shots and screwdrivers. I think she always thought that someday I'd grow up and reach her level of maturity, and then we'd finally get along. When I finally had a Lab and all the rest.

For better or for worse, that will never happen now. If she can't manage to cry for me, she could at least cry about that.

My mother and father are standing to Oriane's left. I can't believe it: for once in their lives, they're not fighting. I guess they've managed to bury the hatchet for the duration of the funeral. Afterward they'll go their own ways. My mother will rejoice in the thought that my father is aging poorly: he must have gained twenty-five pounds and lost half his hair since the last time she saw him. "No regrets there." My father will shake his head as he leaves, relieved to be rid of the disdainful glances from the woman he somehow spent twenty-two years of his life with.

For now, my father is holding my mother up as she cries conspicuously, since everyone knows nothing is worse than losing a child. I feel bad for my dad because I know he's keeping it all inside. He's in much more pain than my mom. I'm sure he'll miss me more than she will. Of course, since I left Paris, my dad and I haven't been able to regularly enjoy our favorite activities together: playing tennis and going to garage sales in his old jalopy of a car at seven in the morning because "that's when you get the best deals, sweetie!" But he comes to visit us in Brittany regularly. He stays two or three days, sometimes a week. He doesn't mind the drive from Nanterre—he's always loved to drive. I know that he'll miss all the time we spent together just the two of us, time that made our father-daughter bond so strong. He'll miss it just as much as I will.

I'm sorry, Dad.

My eyes dart through the rest of the crowd. The friends Gabriel and I made as a couple. My maternal grandparents. My aunt, who's blowing her nose at regular intervals. Gabriel's parents, who have come to support their son. His mother keeps glancing at Gabriel, her eyes round with concern. She seems afraid he might suddenly collapse and that no one will be there to catch him. His father, who stands a head taller than most of the people gathered, looks straight ahead, as if the cypress trees at the edge of the cemetery were what he'd come to see. My cousin and her boyfriend du jour, who seem to be wondering how they should behave. My coworkers: Pablo, Mehdi, and Sébastien, who look like triplets in their strikingly similar black suits, and Elise, whom I could have done without. At least she's not pretending to be inconsolable; she's just staring at her patent-leather heels. My friend Florence, whom I haven't seen since high school. Gabriel's brothers, Grégoire and Laurent, whose eyes are not glued to their smartphone screens for once. My old college roommates, Arthur and Guillaume. We've managed to keep in touch since I moved to Saint-Malo, despite the two hundred fifty miles between us, because we work in the same field.

About forty people total, in this small cemetery on the outskirts of town. A giant dark-green pine towers over my future grave. I smile; at least they found me a spot in the shade.

And then, of course, there's Gabriel. In the front row, next to the gaping hole in the ground. He stares at the casket with a distraught look on his face. I can tell that he hasn't slept in days. He has dark circles under his eyes, and his beard has grown in since he hasn't bothered to shave. He's dressed in a black suit he usually wears to work, with yet another white shirt—also part of his uniform. He looks so handsome I want to cry. I wish I could stroke his cheek. I can almost imagine the feel of his stubble on my palm.

Gabriel . . .

He clears his throat and the crowd quiets down. Whispers stop. The only sound now is that of sniffling noses, their owners trying to be as discreet as possible. He's not looking at anyone, and when he starts speaking, I know he's talking to me and me alone. He doesn't have any notes, and I can't tell if he learned his speech by heart or if he's improvising.

> Chloé, I won't go on too long; I know that you always hated big speeches. And I'm sure you have better things to do wherever you are than to listen to my monologue. I hope that you're somewhere you can feel the wind blowing, hear the leaves rustling, and watch the waves wash in and out. I hope you're free. Free of all physical constraints. I hope you can fly and be everywhere at once.

> I don't want to tell stories about you or say how much I love you, how much I'll miss you. I don't want to say how unfair it is that life has already taken my better half from me. You know all that. And you would roll your eyes if I got all sentimental and poetic. If I let myself go and felt sorry for myself and for you.

> I'll survive, Chloé. Because I know that if I didn't, your disappointment would be much greater than the grief I feel today.

I nod. Gabriel knows me so well. He knew just what to say without making everyone get all weepy. He steps back. They're about to lower the casket into the concrete hole.

From the corner of my eye, I notice a dark figure approaching. He's walking fast, forcing himself not to run, to avoid being noticed by my grieving loved ones as they reflect on Gabriel's words. Despite his efforts, his labored breathing gives him away and curious heads begin to turn.

Simon, embarrassed and out of breath, has made quite an entrance.

He's late, as usual. I hoped he would come and dreaded it at the same time. A long and ambiguous friendship, ended by a single night when things got out of hand. It was the kind of mistake I should have seen coming from miles away, the climax to months of strange tension with Simon. I had played with fire, fanned it, but I always thought I was in control, that I could put an end to it all at any moment and pretend to be an innocent young woman looking for nothing more than a friend.

The story is so common it's pathetic: a one-night stand that wasn't even worth all those weeks spent secretly fantasizing about it. Barely half an hour of lust. I got dressed right afterward and fled the scene as fast as I could. Because I knew immediately that I had made a mistake—somewhere inside I had always known, but the pull of the unfamiliar and the forbidden had been overpowering. I knew that our easy friendship was about to give way to awkwardness and embarrassment because I had stepped over a line I had promised myself never to cross. I felt guilty even before I put my bra back on.

I never saw Simon again. I pushed him out of my life without so much as an explanation. Gabriel never suspected anything, but I decided it was better not to be tempted again, not to have to come face-to-face with my mistake. I knew my husband would never have been able to forgive me for my mistake, and I felt that my unrelenting guilt was punishment enough for my stupid lapse in judgement.

Simon whispers, "Sorry, sorry . . ." as he makes his way through the mourners around my grave. Some of them glare at him in outrage, but they all move out of his way to let him pass.

He must think a funeral is like a rock concert: best from the front row.

GABRIEL

When Gabriel turns around and notices the guy wearing black skinny jeans and a plain white T-shirt and breathing heavily, he wonders if the fatigue from all his sleepless nights is playing tricks on him. He has to be hallucinating. It can't be him. Not only did he dare to show up, but he couldn't even be on time?

What's his name again?

Simon. As if Gabriel could forget. With his black Ray-Bans dangling from his collar, all he needs is a leather jacket slung over his shoulder for people to mistake him for James Dean. The ladies' man. The Don Juan who almost ruined his relationship.

When Gabriel met Chloé in 2005, she had been living in a shabby two-bedroom apartment in Paris with two college friends—Arthur and Guillaume—for a couple of years. All three of them were sports science majors and shared a passion for everything fitness related. When they first started dating and Chloé would have him over for dinner at her place, Gabriel often felt left out of their conversations about training plans, progress, and performance. But she had an amazing way of answering her roommates while looking directly into Gabriel's eyes, as if she were really talking to him, daring him to look away or blush, as if he were the only person at the table who mattered to her. In those moments Gabriel suddenly felt like he and Chloé were alone in the world. Though they could still hear her friends' muffled voices, they seemed to be very far away. The way she looked at him was . . . He still can't find the words to describe her gaze. But every time it made him want to jump out of his chair, grab Chloé by the hand, and leave the table as quickly as possible. He wanted her, of course, but it was more than that: he had an inexplicable feeling that she was made for him, and that, maybe, he was made for her too. When Chloé suggested they move in together just a few months after they met, Gabriel felt like he had won. She had chosen him, yet again.

Chloé finished school, and they spent most of the summer looking for an affordable one-bedroom in the city. She quickly got a job at a gym; Gabriel had already been working for more than a year in a branch office of a big bank. She had just turned twenty-two and he was twenty-four.

Chloé stayed in touch with her former roommates, running with them two or three times a week. They had a hard time replacing her, especially since they weren't students anymore and were looking for a roommate in the same situation. Chloé had felt bad, of course, and had even offered to keep paying her part of the rent until they found someone, but the boys refused. In October, they finally found the gem of a roommate they'd been looking for. His name was Simon.

He was athletic too, but had chosen not to make a career out of it. He was a cook in a small brasserie Gabriel's uncle owned, and planned on eventually becoming a well-known chef. Right after Gabriel met Simon and then introduced the three, it occurred to the boys that in addition to seeming easy enough to get along with, he would probably be willing to make dinner for them every night (a terrible miscalculation on their part, of course, since Simon was usually working in the evenings).

Chloé hit it off with Simon right away, and before long he was running with the three of them regularly. Then, as Arthur and Guillaume became less available—and enthusiastic—about exercising early in the morning before heading to their jobs, Chloé started running alone with the budding chef.

Over the years, Chloé and Simon became close friends. Gabriel didn't worry about any of it; there was no reason to. Simon was the kind of guy everyone liked as soon as he opened his mouth. His charm worked equally well on men and women. While he jumped from girl to girl without getting attached, Chloé and Gabriel were going strong. The perfect couple.

And then, in early 2010, just a few months before their wedding, Simon disappeared from Chloé's life. She started running alone during the week and sometimes met up with Arthur and Guillaume on the weekend. Simon didn't call anymore or show up unannounced at their apartment with a good bottle of wine. After a few weeks, Gabriel asked Chloé if something had happened to him. She casually answered that he'd gotten a new job in a Michelin-starred restaurant and that he was always working. He hardly even had time to eat between the hundreds of plates he prepared during his shift!

Gabriel didn't ask any more questions.

He did notice, however, that Simon immediately RSVP'd to the wedding invitation Chloé had sent, checking the "unable to attend" box for the April celebration. He also picked up on the fact that while Arthur and Guillaume still came over for dinner regularly, Simon either wasn't invited or couldn't make it. And Chloé never hung out at her old apartment with her former roommates anymore.

Gabriel never asked his fiancée about it, but he knew that Simon's total disappearance from her life could only mean one thing. They had gone too far. Once, twice, three times—it hardly mattered. And if Chloé had stopped seeing him, she must have regretted her mistake.

He watched as she planned the wedding, which was getting closer and closer, pulling her hair out over the seating arrangements, choosing the decorations, tasting the dishes that would be served. And he noticed her looking through rental ads for an apartment or small house in Saint-Malo, where they were moving in September. She regularly remarked excitedly, "Can you believe the square footage we're going to be able to get for what we're paying for our one-bedroom in Paris?"

She had agreed to move to Saint-Malo because of the ocean. But she had also agreed to it because once there, Simon would be in the past—definitively. Gabriel figured all this out without saying a single word, without starting a single argument. He decided to suffer in silence and to forgive Chloé, because he could tell that she hadn't forgiven herself. He let her believe that he didn't suspect a thing.

When Gabriel casually asked his uncle about it, he confirmed that Simon had been hired as a sous-chef at a restaurant in the 12th arrondissement. "It's thanks to me, in part. I used my connections to give him a leg up!" he explained, proud to have a few famous chefs for friends. Gabriel nodded and silently contemplated the spoon he was using to stir his black coffee, a dismal expression on his face. "Is something wrong?" his uncle asked.

Two weeks later, when he somewhat accidentally came across the famous Michelin-starred restaurant that had hired Simon, he saw a small sign in the front window: "Wanted: Sous-chef. Experience required. Position available immediately." As he hurried down into the closest metro stop, a smug grin briefly lit up his features.

Gabriel pushes his memories aside. At the end of the funeral, he walks over to greet Simon. The two men shake hands, and the former lover offers the husband his condolences.

"I was so shocked to hear what had happened . . . Chloé told me she went swimming all the time and loved the ocean. I never would have guessed that she was in the slightest danger. I still wonder how something like this could have happened, how she just drowned . . ."

Gabriel nods. Chloé was still in touch with Simon, apparently. He keeps his mouth shut, but makes a mental note.

People slowly start heading back to their cars, to their lives. Gabriel's parents are the last ones to hug him.

Amélie Antoine

"I want to be alone right now, Mom. I'll meet up with you in a bit, okay?"

His mother agrees and strokes his cheek, giving him a supportive look.

Gabriel is now alone in the deserted cemetery, contemplating the grave covered in flowers. His preoccupied gaze focuses on the golden letters that stand out from the dark-gray marble. *Chloé Hamon. 1983–2013.*

So Simon was still in the picture. What else had his wife hidden from him? What other skeletons were destined to come out of the closet now that she was gone?

EMMA

I liked Edith Adelstein right away and I think the feeling was mutual. She must be used to having retirees as volunteers and think that a bit of youthful energy will be good for her association. New ideas and some initiative.

Coping with Bereavement—CWB for those in the know—offers the bereft a chance to share their experience, their pain, and their memories in group sessions led by specially trained volunteers. Edith has agreed to move forward with my idea of helping any interested participants make a memorial album for the loved ones they've lost. The process of going back through all the photos, selecting the most important ones, and maybe having me enhance the chosen portraits could be a great way to help the participants get through the mourning process.

She suggested that I be a part of the next group, which is scheduled to start in about a month and a half. The number of participants is deliberately kept quite small so that they each have a chance to express themselves and foster meaningful relationships with one another as the sessions go on. There will be five or six mourners, of all ages and from all walks of life. Edith will lead the group to keep an eye on me. That's not how she put it, but that's what I understood. She's afraid I'll put my foot in my mouth since this will be my first experience with bereavement and I haven't had any special training. I'll attend the group as an observer only and will work with participants who choose to create the memorial albums outside of the monthly meetings.

The group's first meeting is scheduled for July 8. Until then, I have plenty to do given the scope of the project for the Saint-Malo tourism office. They want pictures of every square inch of the city and want me to take advantage of every single minute of sunshine to capture the Breton town in its best light.

I decide to get my DSLR ready for a little excursion out on the levee. It's not particularly nice out, but the light is perfect for photographing the breakwaters. It's seven in the evening, and I'm hoping that the beach will be deserted this late in the day. There's nothing more frustrating than having to wait for people to walk out of the frame of the picture you're trying to take . . .

My cell phone rings and the sound of "Where Is My Mind?" by the Pixies resonates through my little studio. I glance quickly at the screen: it's my mother. Again. She has a gift for always calling at the wrong time. I answer with a sigh because this is the third time she's tried to reach me since I got here, and she'll worry and maybe even call the Saint-Malo police and local hospitals if I don't pick up.

"Hello, Emma? It's Mom! I was starting to worry! I've left you several messages since Friday. You could have called me back, you know. I know you must be *very* busy, but I can't imagine you couldn't find five minutes to pick up the phone . . ."

My mother emphasizes the "very" to make her sarcasm obvious and let me know I've hurt her feelings by not calling.

"I know, Mom, I'm sorry. I had to clean the studio top to bottom as soon as I arrived, then unpack and meet with the tourism office and bereavement association, so I haven't had a single minute to myself. I was just about to head out to take a few pictures of the beach."

"So, what you're trying to say is that—as usual—I'm inconveniencing you, right?"

"No, Mom, don't flip out on me! You always twist everything I say. I just wanted to tell you what I've spent the weekend doing, that's all . . ."

I can feel that this is yet another conversation that's going to turn into a list of grievances: I never call; I chose to move to the other side of the country for no reason; I never take her advice; etc. Why is everything always so hard with my mom?

"I'll call you sometime this week, okay? And I'll e-mail you my first photos if you want. Okay, bye, Mom. Love you."

My mother grumbles something, then hangs up. I know that she'll go moan and complain to my father, who'll reply, "Give the girl some space! She's not fifteen anymore."

I add Edith to my list of contacts, which is quite short. I only include people I actually call: my mother, my father, and my brother, Nathan, of course. My maternal grandparents' landline, even though I call them much less than I should. My hairdresser, though I'll have to find a new one in Saint-Malo. Louis, an old college friend from Arles. Not really a friend anymore, more of a colleague. He also takes wedding pictures. The only difference is that it's enough for him. We still sometimes call each other to share ideas or discuss equipment. My banker. I don't call him, but having his number in my contacts means that I know when he's calling, usually to talk about my overdrawn account. This way I can transfer enough money to keep him at bay without actually having to talk to him.

I don't have a best friend to tell all my secrets to or call at two o'clock in the morning if I feel sad or anxious. I don't have a group of friends to call about pulling together a last-minute gathering either. In fact, I'm a loner. I've always been that way and I've never had a problem with it. I like to go to the movies alone, exercise alone, and daydream on my towel at the beach alone. And, of course, I like to be alone with my camera.

When I was little, my worrywart of a mother couldn't stand my preference for solitude and thought there had to be something wrong with me since I never had any friends over. She would occasionally decide it was a good idea to invite the neighbor girl or the son of one of her colleagues over so we could have fun together. Every time, she would find them wandering through the house alone, since I had gone off to have my own fun at the far end of the yard or in the attic. After I explained that I was quite happy to be alone and that I didn't feel especially inclined to have people around, my mother finally gave in.

I don't have a steady boyfriend who will follow me anywhere either. I'm more the kind of girl who has a series of one-night stands and week-long flings. The kind who leaves before the sleeping body next to her wakes up and who always hesitates to give out a real phone number. I don't know how to get close to people. My mother is always saying it's because I haven't met the "right" man yet, but sometimes I wonder if I'm actually incapable of loving anyone. Maybe love is incompatible with my dreams of freedom, of getting away.

I admit that right now I wish I had a best friend to share my doubts and fears with. She could reassure me, tell me that I'm making the right choice, that what's important is living my dream of traveling abroad with my camera in a bag slung over my shoulder. I'm sure it would be more helpful than talking to my reflection in the mirror.

I turn off my phone and place it in my bag with my lenses. I hate to be interrupted when I'm taking pictures.

CHAPTER 5
JUNE 2013

CHLOÉ

I'm starting to lose track of time; the days all run together. But I know I've been dead for over a month.

I watch as Gabriel wanders aimlessly around our home.

The first week, he didn't even poke his head outside. He lazed around the house, near comatose, like a zombie. I felt like I was watching a scene from *The Walking Dead*. He hardly ate a thing, but drank a lot. He slept all day and spent his nights zoning out in front of the TV, the circles under his eyes darkening every day.

The second week, he spent most of his time crying. He started up any time he came across one of my belongings—which of course translates to about half the objects in the house. Tears started rolling at the sight of my electric kettle and tea bags; he sobbed in front of my sandals at the foot of the stairs. He fell to pieces when he noticed the half-read novel on my nightstand and wiped his eyes when he received letters addressed to me. I sighed as I watched him smell my pillow night after night. It got old pretty quickly.

The third week, he accidentally knocked over a gilded glass vase he had given me when we moved into the house in Saint-Malo. After studying the pieces strewn all over the white tile floor with a tormented look on his face, he suddenly fell into a terrible rage. He hurled anything and everything he could get his hands on at the walls: potted plants, dishes from the counter, and even books from the shelves. And he did it all without making a sound, not a single scream or groan. He only stopped after grabbing a framed photo of the two of us on vacation in Spain. Gabriel slid down the wall, out of breath, and put the frame down next to him, then rested his head in his hands and started crying—obviously.

All that for a vase I didn't even really like.

I wish I could tell him he's not allowed to just let himself *drown* in grief like that—the metaphor is just too easy. He has to get ahold of himself; he has no choice.

A few days after this incomprehensible scene, he went back to work. I think that Geoffrey helped by constantly calling and knocking on the door. I sighed with relief. Gabriel went back to a normal schedule: he got up in the morning, went to work, and slept at night. I mean, he wasn't exactly bursting with energy, and he ordered pizza every night, but at least he wasn't letting himself waste away anymore. I thought he might even realize what a mess the house was before long . . .

The fourth week, it was back to square one. Gabriel started listening to "Ain't No Sunshine" on repeat—the song we'd chosen for our first dance. We'd savored it, locked in a tender embrace, as if we'd been the only people there. When Bill Withers belted, "This house just ain't no home any time she goes away," for the fifty-seventh time, I wanted to scream. Sure, Gabriel loves me. And sure, he misses me. But there's no point in going overboard. Why wallow in it?

It's true that in some ways I'm flattered to see him in such a state. I don't want him to forget me and move on. If he weren't in pain, I would be. But I also need to see that he's a fighter. A man. I've always been like that; I can't stand weakness. If I could, I'd grab him by the shoulders and give him a good shake. And I'd hand him a razor while I was at it—so he could get rid of the fuzzy beard that's covering half his face, of course, not for anything else.

I want him to be miserable without me, but a strong, masculine miserable.

This week he's started putting away my clothes. I think it's a bit early, but maybe he read somewhere that he should do it, or maybe his mom told him that sorting through my closet would help him clear some things out of his head. She's an expert when it comes to bogus bits of wisdom like that.

First he took my yellow dress—the one I had planned to wear to dinner at his parents' (which reminds me: at least I got out of that)—off the hanger. He carefully placed it in a big box he must have bought for the occasion. Then he put all my jeans in, pair by pair, sighing at regular intervals. My sweaters, button-up shirts, and dresses. My workout clothes, my bathing suits—except for the black one I was wearing the day of. My whole wardrobe. The only thing he kept was a large turquoise silk shawl, one of his favorites. He held it to his nose for a few moments, then tucked it away in the drawer of his nightstand. He closed the three boxes he had filled with brown packing tape, then placed them on the highest shelf in the closet. I admit I don't understand what the point is. I thought he was going to donate my clothes, or maybe sell them, given the price tag for some of my dresses! Not just put them all back in the closet. But his mother often has strange ideas; that must be the explanation.

He ran his fingers over the cover of the novel lying on my nightstand, but didn't put it in the drawer.

Next, he threw out everything of mine in the bathroom. My toothbrush, my makeup, my lotions and toners, my bubble bath, my razor, my hair ties. Even my perfume. He opened the little wooden box where

I kept my jewelry, seemed to hesitate, then closed it and pushed it to the back of the cabinet.

Finally, he tied up the big garbage bag and sat on the edge of the bathtub. He stayed there for a few minutes, totally motionless. I have no idea what he was thinking. He didn't seem all that sad, more wistful.

It broke my heart to see him like that, even if he had just thrown out an almost new bottle of YSL Parisienne.

GABRIEL

Gabriel spends the morning at the morgue picking up Chloé's wedding ring and bracelet. Once home, he puts the bracelet away in the bathroom and slides her ring onto the chain he wears around his neck. He slips it under his T-shirt, where it will be safe from the sympathetic glances he just can't take any longer.

The police also gave him back her car keys and her purse, both of which they'd found inside her car. Her Renault Clio was still sitting where she'd parked it before going swimming. Gabriel will have his father bring it to the house; he can't bear to do it himself. He'll ask Geoffrey to sell it online.

He opens Chloé's purse and takes out its hidden treasures one by one. A box of mint Tic Tacs. Her house keys. A tube of lip gloss. A pocket mirror. An old pen with a chewed-up cap. A wallet filled with dozens of rewards cards, a five-euro bill, and an old photo-booth portrait of Gabriel. Two hair ties and a black barrette.

And her phone. Gabriel turns it on and enters her PIN: four zeros. Chloé never understood why it was important to have a secret password. The screen comes to life. Seven text messages and five voice messages. Gabriel erases them one by one after checking that they're all from him.

He opens Chloé's contacts and scrolls directly to the letter *S*. A single entry: Simon. So she didn't erase him. Or she re-entered his number. Gabriel keeps telling himself a phone number doesn't mean anything, but he feels betrayed.

He browses through old texts on the SIM card.

Mom: "It would be nice if you'd call me every once in a while!"

Oriane: "Sorry to ask this now, but do you think the kids could stay over at your place on Friday night? I'd come get them Saturday morning . . ."

Mehdi: "Can we trade classes: your Wednesday Pilates for my Thursday morning step aerobics?"

No messages from Simon—unless they'd been erased.

Gabriel is not proud of how obsessed he's become with the guy since he saw him at Chloé's funeral, but he can't get the doubt and suspicion out of his head. He needs to know if he was right to forgive his wife. He needs to know that she really loved him, now that she's not here to tell him herself.

He dumps everything back into her purse and puts it in the drawer of the coffee table. He also puts away the official version of the autopsy report, which they gave him this morning with Chloé's jewelry. He hasn't even opened the envelope. Why bother? Gabriel already knows what's inside. The coroner called him three weeks ago to share his findings. He concluded, from the cerebral hemorrhage he'd found during the autopsy, that Chloé had had an aneurism and drowned as a result. The coroner's explanation cleared up the one question Gabriel hadn't been able to answer: how his wife, an experienced swimmer, had drowned in a calm sea.

The rest isn't important. Chloé is gone. Period.

Gabriel notices the brochure a funeral home employee handed him the day Chloé was buried. *Coping with Bereavement: You don't have to do it alone.* The man had slipped it into his hand before leaving the cemetery with the hearse.

"I know this isn't a good time, but this association really helped me when I lost my brother a few years ago. I had plenty of reservations about group therapy, but I met some really great people. People who understood me because they were going through the same thing . . ."

To be polite, Gabriel had put the leaflet in his pocket instead of throwing it in the first trash can he could find. Spilling his guts to strangers wasn't his thing. He hardly confided in his friends and family, much less people he didn't even know.

But now he has to admit that he's drowning on his own. He feels different from everyone else, his suffering immeasurable and incomprehensible. He's back at work, he sees friends, he has dinner with his parents, but he knows a part of him died with Chloé.

Going through her things didn't help, despite his mother's suggestion that it would.

He wants to scream all the time. He's angry at everyone for no reason. He collapses in tears as soon as no one's looking, and he isn't interested in or excited about anything. He drags through every day, trying to keep up appearances behind a fake smile.

He's tired of pretending.

He could always give it a try—if he doesn't like it, he won't go back.

His train of thought is suddenly interrupted when someone knocks firmly on the front door. Gabriel trudges over and opens it to find Geoffrey with his fist still in the air.

"I wasn't sure you could hear me," he offers awkwardly as an excuse.

"It would be nice if you'd learn that nowadays people use doorbells. Your knuckles are going to leave a permanent mark on the door if you keep this up."

Gabriel opens the door all the way, then heads back to the living room without a second glance at his best friend. Geoffrey falls in behind him.

"Not so fast, buddy! I have a present for you. I was thinking that since you don't want to hang out with me right now, it would still do you some good to have *someone* to keep you company . . ."

Gabriel turns around and notices a dog sitting quietly on the front stoop, waiting to be invited in.

"What the hell is that?" he mutters as his eyebrows lower into a frown.

"A dog!" replies Geoffrey, clearly thrilled with his surprise.

"Yes, I can see it's a dog, thank you. But what is he doing here exactly?"

"I just told you. He'll keep you company since you don't want to see anyone. Think about it: you don't even have to make small talk for him to like you! I know you've always wanted a dog, so don't try to tell me otherwise. It's the perfect time to adopt one."

"But Chloé . . ."

Gabriel stops. Chloé would never have wanted a dog. But she's gone now.

Geoffrey is quiet. He doesn't know what to say, can't find the right words to comfort his friend.

Gabriel contemplates the cream-colored golden retriever. The dog stares back without moving. It seems like he's waiting for his potential new master to make up his mind.

He almost got a dog once, nearly twenty years ago. A mutt, with black fur and ears almost as big as a fox's. He happened upon him on his way home from middle school, on the deserted dirt path he always used as a shortcut. He can still see the way the dog sat with his head tilted to one side, as if he'd been waiting. He bent down to pet him, and when he started walking again, the stray fell in behind him without a second thought. Gabriel tried to shoo him away several times, but it was no use. When the pair reached home, he glanced at the dog and said, "Wait here." He received a hushed bark in reply, interpreted as agreement.

Gabriel's mother refused to agree, however. There was no way they were going to adopt a dog, especially not some mutt he'd found in the street. "We don't even know where he came from! And what about your brother?"

His father mumbled that he didn't care one way or the other, that Gabriel would have to work it out with his mother. So the boy put on the cutest smile he could manage and cajolingly begged her, "Pretty please, my wonderful, beautiful mommy, please, please, please say yes! Grégoire won't mind. Just look at him, he's such a good dog, and he's so little too!" His mother finally gave in with a shrug, and Gabriel brought the dog into the house, promising to take him out for walks and that she wouldn't have to take care of him at all.

But his younger brother, Grégoire, screamed as soon as he came down from his room. He had been terrified of dogs since he was a baby, though no one knew why. Gabriel tried to reassure him: the dog barely reached his knees and hadn't even growled! But there was no point. Grégoire ran back up to his room to hide, unwilling to discuss the subject. Their mother got upset, and then their father got involved. By the time Laurent, the oldest brother, got home from school, the house was like a war zone.

"I told you bringing a dog home was a bad idea!"

"No, I think it's a great idea and a chance for your son to stop acting like such a wimp!" rallied their father, annoyed that he couldn't read the newspaper in peace.

Gabriel knew that any subject would do when it came to starting a fight between his parents. They loved arguing and especially loved making up afterward. They never thought twice about the consequences of imposing such a stressful environment on their children.

Grégoire refused to come down to the kitchen that evening and instead ate dinner in his room. Gabriel and Laurent stared at their plates to avoid becoming collateral damage as their parents continued to scream at one another. The dog sat silently in the entryway without moving a muscle.

The next morning, Gabriel left early with the dog, who eagerly followed him, happy to get out of the house. He walked for at least an hour through the Breton countryside, the dog on his heels and his hands in his pockets.

When he finally stopped, he looked at the mutt and told him to go. The dog didn't move.

"I said go! I can't keep you. You get that, don't you?"

The dog tilted his head to the side with a whine.

"Get out of here, all right? You already messed everything up last night!"

Suddenly unable to contain his anger, Gabriel picked up a handful of rocks and started pelting the dog, who finally got the message. When he got home, nobody mentioned the previous evening's incident or asked what had happened to the dog. That day, Gabriel gave up on the idea of ever having a dog again.

Now, Gabriel looks at Geoffrey and scratches his head, perplexed. "He doesn't look like a young pup."

"I got him at the Humane Society. I thought it would be better not to bring you a puppy who still pees on the floor that you'd have to house-train. He's six years old. The lady told me he's very sociable, so I thought he'd make up for your shortcomings in that department."

"Ha ha." Gabriel kneels down and pets the dog's head. "He'll get hair all over everything."

"But Chloé's not here anymore," Geoffrey says without thinking. He bites his lower lip, flustered. "Um, what I mean is . . ."

"You're right. Chloé's gone," Gabriel replies gently.

"His name is Lucky. You can change it, but I'm not sure he'll understand that you're talking to him."

Gabriel and Lucky measure each other up in silence. Maybe it's a sign that a dog turned up on his doorstep like this, by surprise.

The dog instinctively tilts his head to the side.

Geoffrey can tell it's a done deal and makes a discreet exit.

EMMA

"Are you sure you don't want it somewhere a little less conspicuous? Have you really thought about this? I assume you know that there's no going back!"

"I'm sure. Don't worry."

The tattoo artist, a young woman with bright-red hair, nods and shows me the stencil she's going to use on the inside of my wrist. An eagle with open wings spanning two inches. The design is exactly what I'd imagined: she's drawn a stylized black bird of prey. Simple and understated, with sleek lines.

While quickly disinfecting my skin, she asks why I chose this design. Probably more to be polite than out of actual interest, but I answer anyway.

"Freedom and sharp eyes. So I don't forget who I want to be. So I remember to break out of my cage and stay true to my point of view."

My words sound pretty trite, but I don't know how else to explain my choice. The tattoo artist offers up an unconvincing "mmm hmm." She must be used to pseudophilosophical speeches and bogus symbolism. It doesn't matter. What's important is that it means something to me.

She concentrates as she places the stencil on my wrist and starts to trace it. I clench my teeth. I knew that I'd chosen a sensitive area, but I wasn't prepared for quite this much pain. I exhale slowly. I focus on the electric needle; with each passing minute it reveals more and more of the eagle's outstretched wings.

After half an hour, the tattoo artist wipes my wrist with a piece of cloth, disinfects my skin again, and applies a kind of transparent film. It's done.

"Don't forget to apply Neosporin for the next two weeks. And feel free to come back if you need a touch-up."

The redhead is already thinking about something else. Her next customer is clearly a regular: a walking canvas. I study the blue veins that are visible under the jet-black eagle. The tattoo artist clears her throat to signal that it's time for me to go. Her day has only just started, and she still has quite a few dolphins, stars, and Chinese characters to inscribe on the skin of various strangers.

I hurry to pick up my bag and jacket, then open the door and leave the tattoo parlor. I have to go to the pharmacy, and then I need to . . .

All of a sudden, something runs into my leg and I lose my balance. I try to steady myself, but despite my efforts I end up flat on my butt. I glance down the sidewalk to see a beige blur moving quickly away.

"Come back here, Lucky! Come back here right now! Luckyyyyy!"

Two legs in a pair of black pants stop in front of me. I look up to see a man in his thirties, looking terribly apologetic as he holds out his hand.

"I'm really so sorry . . . My dog doesn't listen . . . I've only had him for a few days and it's a lot of work. He takes advantage of every second I'm not paying attention to yank on the leash and run off. Are you all right?"

He helps me to my feet, and I brush off my jeans. I open my bag to make sure my camera is still in one piece. The man is standing in front of me, arms dangling. He rubs the back of his head awkwardly as he subtly glances behind me to where the dog disappeared. He must be long gone by now.

"I'm okay, don't worry about it," I say with a polite smile.

He seems relieved.

"You can go now," I offer.

"Go where?"

"Um, to get your dog . . ."

"Oh. Yes, of course. Thank you . . ."

The stranger suddenly takes off at a run. When he reaches the corner, he doesn't seem to know which way to go. He turns his head both ways, an undecided expression on his face. The dog is nowhere to be found. After a few seconds, he decides to go left. He looks back a last time to wave at me, as if to say, "Again, so sorry!"

After I stop in the pharmacy to get the ointment for my tattoo, I go back to my place. The days are long; time seems to have slowed down, despite the fact that I'm plenty busy. I finished the project for the tourism office in just three weeks. The first session for the new bereavement group will be held in a little over a week. All my weekends are booked for weddings and maternity shoots. I've already erased my fair share of stretch marks and under-eye circles with Photoshop, but a job's a job for now . . .

I guess it's because I still don't know anyone here that time drags on and on. I like being alone, it's true, but I realize now that I'm not cut out for being alone all the time. Like everyone, I guess.

CHAPTER 6
JULY 2013

CHLOÉ

The first time I ever saw Gabriel, he was standing on the sidewalk out-side the Société Générale branch on Boulevard de Magenta. He was leaning against the bank's glass storefront smoking a cigarette with a pensive look on his face, his right hand in the pocket of his black suit pants. His curly brown hair fell just above his eyes; he reminded me of the singer Mika.

Mika in a suit, I guess. Before he cut his hair.

Anyway . . .

I walked by him at top speed because I was running late for lunch with a friend. A few yards past him, I turned around to look, but kept walking. *Not bad.* He hadn't even noticed me. I slowed down without really thinking, then stopped. I hesitated: Sara would not be happy. I could already imagine her pouty face, hurt that I'd made her wait for so long yet again. I quickly pushed that unhappy thought out of my head; I was sure I'd be able to appease her with details about the man I was about to meet.

I casually walked past him again, more slowly, so I'd have time to get a better look. *More than not bad.* About twenty-five years old, tall and thin, broad shoulders. A five-o'clock shadow he would probably shave the next morning. But beyond all that, he exuded something indescribable, a blend of calmness and nonchalance, a kind of detached serenity. The type of man who doesn't know he's attractive and who looks at you with wide eyes when you express interest.

He still hadn't noticed me; he seemed completely absorbed in his thoughts. Oh well. I decided to take the first step for once.

I was considering what to say to get his attention when he suddenly stubbed out his cigarette, glanced at his watch, and walked back into the bank. My prey had disappeared before I'd managed to say a single word. There was no way I was going to admit defeat. Sara could wait a few more minutes.

I went into the branch and walked over to the pimple-faced receptionist sorting checkbooks.

"I'd like to make an appointment with the account manager who just came in."

"Okay, to do what?"

"Uh, to open a checking account."

"I can open one for you right now, miss. You don't need an appointment for that!" replied the young man politely as he pushed his glasses back up his incredibly greasy nose.

"I'd rather see an account manager. I plan to transfer all my savings, and I need to know what kinds of investments would be best," I answered more abruptly. The receptionist didn't need to know that, at twenty-two, my savings totaled about seven hundred euros and were vegetating in a low-interest savings account opened when I'd turned eighteen.

"All right, miss. I can get you an appointment with Mr. Hamon tomorrow morning at nine fifteen. Would that work for you?"

"That's perfect. That's the man who just walked in, right?"

"Yes, that's him."

The employee gazed at me with an inquisitive frown on his face, but I decided not to explain myself. I had a lunch to get to.

I met Gabriel—Mr. Hamon—the next morning. I took extra time to get ready and primp. I wanted to do myself up in a way that made me look naturally elegant. A pair of dark-blue skinny jeans, a tailored ivory blouse, and ankle boots.

He invited me into his office at nine fifteen on the dot. He asked for my first and last name, address, etc. He meticulously filled out his file, hardly even glancing at me.

This wasn't going to be easy.

We talked about checking accounts, debit cards, checkbooks, and sustainable development investment accounts. He didn't even blink when I told him my fortune only totaled about seven hundred euros.

"Don't forget the interest!" I added with a laugh.

He didn't smile.

After about thirty minutes, I'd blown through my stock of relevant questions, and he closed my file with a satisfied look on his face.

"I'll handle the transfer of accounts with your current bank so you don't have to, Ms. Vasseur."

He seemed to be waiting for me to get up, shake his hand, and leave.

"And . . . um . . . do you have plans for lunch today?" I ventured.

The words just popped out, unannounced, the product of my desperation.

"I'll check my schedule, but you don't need to make an appointment to bring in the papers we discussed," he said, clicking the calendar icon on his computer screen.

"No, I meant . . . would you like to have lunch with me?"

I was usually so sure of myself, but I was fumbling. My voice seemed almost shy.

He looked up and stared at me without a word, clearly confused. I had plenty of time to study his surprised green eyes. The silence became awkward, so I stood up and smiled.

"It was just an idea, you know. Forget it."

I started to make my retreat. He didn't move. I opened the door to leave, hoping that he'd come after me. I felt so humiliated!

He didn't say anything.

The door closed behind me, and I rushed through the branch to the front entrance.

"Have a nice day, miss," said the receptionist.

I stepped through the door and found myself back in the street at last. I sighed loudly as I started down the boulevard without looking back. What a disaster!

My phone rang in the bottom of my purse. Unknown number.

"Hello," I answered coldly. It wasn't a good time to try and sell me a new Internet subscription or ask me to answer a survey.

"Yes."

"What?"

"Yes, I'd like to have lunch with you."

GABRIEL

"I don't want to start at the end. I want to tell you about when Chloé was still here, because that's what's hardest now. Living without her. I still remember the first time she walked past me. She must have thought I hadn't even noticed her: I did my best to seem indifferent. But really, I just lacked self-confidence. I'm sure I never would have worked up the courage to talk to her myself. So when I saw her walk into my office the next morning, I was a mess. And when she asked me to have lunch with her, I thought I would turn into a puddle on the floor. She must have thought it was all indifference and nonchalance when in fact it was awkwardness and nerves. She was the kind of girl who scared men off with her confidence. But over time, I think I managed to tame her. I pierced through her shell, her arrogant armor, to find a generous and loving woman. Moody and stubborn too, however, I won't deny that . . ."

Gabriel smiles. He sees Chloé doing her hair in the bathroom mirror. Her determined expression as she tried to arrange it into the perfect bun, her annoyed sighs every time a strand refused to be tamed. "My hair is impossible!" The way she carefully applied her eyeliner right along the lash line, her mouth slightly ajar. And how she would push him away lovingly—but firmly—when he took advantage of her concentration to kiss her neck. "Just give me five minutes! You're going to ruin it!" The annoyed face she would make when he ignored her. "Be patient, we'll have plenty of time later . . ."

We'll have plenty of time . . .

And her laugh, when she finally gave in, with the contours of a single eye traced in black. Her laugh when she kissed him and he could feel her teeth against his lips. Her laugh when she jumped into his arms and wrapped her legs around his waist so he could take her wherever he liked.

Her laugh.

Gabriel absentmindedly clenches his jaw. He's not looking at anyone; he seems lost in his memories. Then, all of a sudden, he startles back to reality. He looks up and realizes that everyone is staring at him. At least it's done now; he's opened up to total strangers. Not the whole story, of course, but he's started to let them in. He doesn't know why, but he feels safe.

There are eight of them in all. Edith, who leads the group; a volunteer photographer named Emma; and five other mourners like himself (he hates the word "mourner" but that's what they say in the group): Gisèle, a woman not far from retirement who just lost her husband; Oscar, a twenty-something student whose mother committed suicide several years ago; Michel, an old bachelor crushed by his father's death; Laura, a woman a bit older than Gabriel who lost her husband in a motorcycle accident; and Marie-Hélène, a mother grieving her son, who died of leukemia at just seventeen.

Edith explained how the group works at the beginning of the meeting. One session a month for a year, each of which examines a particular theme. The participants commit to attending all the sessions out of respect for the others. Everything that is said in front of the group stays with the group. They are free to speak or not, but they all have to listen without passing judgement.

Emma talks to them about putting together memorial albums, and it occurs to Gabriel that despite everything he's put away, he hasn't even thought to go through the photo albums in the living room bookcase.

Next the participants introduce themselves one by one. They briefly explain who they lost and each of them lights a candle, which they'll blow out at the end of the session. Some of them cry. Others seem to be reciting lines they've learned by heart—probably just a different reaction to the stress. Gabriel thought he would say as little as possible, but found himself going back almost eight years to nostalgically tell the story of the first time he met Chloé.

It's Marie-Hélène's turn to talk. She's shaking with hesitation. Gabriel almost wants to hold her hand. The words won't come out; her emotions are too overwhelming.

"It's okay," says Edith. "Take all the time you need; we're not in a rush. And if you don't want to talk now, you can wait till you feel up to it."

Everyone is so understanding and encouraging that Marie-Hélène sighs, as if an unbearable weight has just been lifted off her shoulders, then begins to speak. "Sacha's been gone for three months already." She shakes her head and lets out a sad laugh. "When I say 'gone,' I mean dead."

The air grows heavy with the weight of the word.

"After months of treatments and suffering, my first reaction when he closed his eyes for the last time in his hospital bed was relief. I was relieved for him, of course, but also for me. The unbearable wait was finally over. I felt awful . . . And for three months now, it's like I've been underwater. My lungs ready to burst, silence and darkness all around me. I want to scream, and I feel like I'm just letting myself sink, slowly but surely. I keep thinking that I'll eventually reach the bottom, and then I'll be able to come back up to the surface . . . But I just keep sinking, deeper and deeper."

Gabriel looks over at Marie-Hélène, who has stopped talking. The words she's just spoken could have been his own, and probably those of all the other people sitting around the oval table. He exchanges a glance with Emma, who's seated across from him. She smiles faintly, but he can see that her eyes are red.

He hears Edith talking again, though she sounds very far away.

"Thank you all for coming together to create this safe space, for agreeing to listen to each other and share your pain. When you're ready, you can blow out your candles . . . The next session will focus on memories. In the month between now and the next time we see each other, I'd like you to think about the happiest memories you have of the person who is no longer with you . . ."

Gabriel blows on the flame of his candle, which flickers and goes out. He runs his finger over his wife's name, written in chalk on the small slate candleholder. He walks out into the cool night air and lights a cigarette on the porch, where he's sheltered from the wind. Chloé would be furious if she knew he'd started smoking again. There are extenuating circumstances, though . . . "That's no excuse!" He can almost hear her voice laden with reproach.

The photographer comes out of the room and walks past him, car keys in hand. Then she turns around and says, "So, did you find him?"

Gabriel looks at her, uncomprehending.

"Your dog, did you find him?"

Now he recognizes the young woman Lucky knocked over a few weeks ago.

"Oh, I'm sorry, I didn't recognize you . . . Yes, yes, I found him, and, more importantly, I've managed to teach him to stay on a leash!"

Gabriel smiles. He wants to keep talking, to avoid being alone with his thoughts, but he doesn't know quite what to say.

"Your memorial album idea, how would it work exactly? I have a bunch of photo albums at home, but I haven't had the strength to open a single one. I'm afraid it will hurt too much, that it's too soon, that it'll bring back too many memories . . ."

"I understand. The idea would be to choose about a dozen photos of your wife from among all the pictures you have. The ones that mean the most to you. I can work on them so they'll look good together. And when it's done, you could present it at a group session. But if it's too soon . . ."

"I want to do it," Gabriel interrupts. "I doubt I'll ever be strong enough to go through all the albums on my own."

Emma nods gently.

EMMA

I hear barking as soon as I ring the doorbell, far away at first, then getting closer. I step back.

Gabriel cracks the door as he holds the golden retriever with one hand to keep him from darting out.

"Please, come in."

I walk down the hallway and stop at the entrance to the living room. Gabriel gestures to the couch and I notice a pile of albums on the coffee table. We spend an hour going through the pages together, watching as eight years fly by. Gabriel doesn't talk much, simply stops me from time to time to show me a picture or tell a story. Sometimes he decides to take a photo from its black page, gently running his index finger under each of the four corners to remove the one he's chosen.

When we're done, he places eight pictures on the coffee table.

A close-up of Chloé that must date back to the beginning of their relationship; she looks like she's in her early twenties. She's smiling, her head resting on her shoulder.

A photo of the two of them that Gabriel must have taken himself, his arm outstretched. He's looking at the camera, his face serious. Chloé's laughing and kissing his cheek.

A shot of Chloé walking on the beach in the distance, her feet in the water. I can't help but notice how well it's framed. She's on the right, the waves slipping away on the left.

Chloé blowing out her birthday candles: twenty-five twinkling little sticks on a huge three-tiered cake.

Another close-up of her making a face for the camera. Her hair is in her face, and she's crossing her eyes and sticking her front teeth out like a squirrel. A bit blurry.

A photo of Chloé drenched in sweat, apparently after a race. She's wearing a black tank top with neon-yellow stripes, and her hair is up in a ponytail. I can tell she's out of breath. She's holding her hand out toward the camera, trying to avoid being photographed.

Chloé in her wedding dress, of course. A strapless dress that complements her tanned shoulders and chest. She's concentrating, studying herself in a full-length mirror, fixing a runaway strand of hair. The last private moment before the ceremony, probably captured by the wedding photographer.

And finally, a picture of her sleeping. A stolen moment. Her long hair flows over the pillow and her face is just barely visible.

I feel like an intruder.

Gabriel looks at the pictures one last time with a satisfied expression on his face, then hands them to me.

"Could you turn it into a black-and-white series? Really heighten the contrast?"

I agree and tell him it shouldn't take long for me to scan them and make the changes. I stand up, put the photos into my bag, and get ready to leave.

"It's almost twelve thirty. We could order sushi if you want. I mean, if you like sushi, obviously. Otherwise we could do pizza? I'd like to be distracted for a while . . ."

"Sushi sounds good. But if we're going to have lunch together, we should probably be on a first-name basis, don't you think?"

Gabriel smiles.

Forty-five minutes later we're sitting at the table in his open kitchen on old bar stools they probably bought at a garage sale. Gabriel asks me if I've been living in Saint-Malo for long, and I tell him about my move from Arles.

He shares all the things he loves about Brittany, the region where he grew up. The dramatic countryside, the raging winds so strong you're sometimes convinced you're really going to fly away, solitary moments on the beach with a kite.

I listen to him talk, simply nodding in encouragement. Lucky is lying on the tile floor next to his master. He also seems to know he shouldn't disturb this happy moment.

Gabriel doesn't say Chloé's name at all, not even once.

CHAPTER 7
AUGUST 2013

CHLOÉ

That dog is really starting to make himself at home. At first he obediently slept in the dog bed Gabriel had put in the kitchen for him. He'd even covered it in an old blanket so it would be nice and cozy for the sweet little doggy.

But now that he's gotten comfortable, the rascal climbs onto the couch whenever Gabriel's watching television. He even goes upstairs. Before long, he'll be sleeping in our bed. And he sheds everywhere, which Gabriel doesn't seem to mind a bit.

"Lucky." What a joke!

If I could strangle Geoffrey for his stupid idea, I would—gleefully.

"I know you've always wanted a dog!"

Whatever. Gabriel never dreamed of having a dog. I would have known, after all. If we'd ever talked about the subject, I would remember.

We had bigger dreams than walking a Labrador every evening and cleaning dog hair off the couch.

Once, early on in the relationship, we made a list of everything we wanted to do before we turned thirty. Our short- and medium-term plans. We spent the whole night on it, with Indian takeout for sustenance.

Having a dog was not on the list.

If I remember right, it went like this: buy an apartment in the Paris metro area (though a few years later we ended up with a rented house in Saint-Malo instead); visit New York City (our honeymoon); and have the most beautiful wedding at a castle with a pond (the pond was optional).

Gabriel hesitantly brought up the possibility of adding a baby to the list, but I laughed and said, "Before we turn thirty? We'll have plenty of time for kids later! There are so many things to experience before then!"

"Yeah, of course. You're right," replied Gabriel. And we never talked about it again. What a crazy idea.

I added skydiving. With or without Gabriel. And, of course, having enough money for finances to never be an obstacle to our plans.

Actually, in just a few years, we managed to accomplish most of our goals. Except for getting rich, but that was more a dream than an actual plan. Or at least that's what I told myself.

I'm thirty years old today. Happy birthday, Chloé.

I'm starting to get a little tired of watching Gabriel get on with his life while I'm stuck here. Waiting, always waiting. It's no way to live—or die, for that matter.

It's probably in poor taste, but the thing I miss most is swimming in the ocean. Concentrating on my regular breathing, the rhythm of the waves, my heartbeat echoing under the water.

And running. Putting in my headphones, cranking the volume all the way up on my MP3 player, and letting my legs rack up mile after mile. Sprinting to Stromae, slowing down to Radiohead, keeping myself going with Christine and the Queens. Passing occasional joggers and nodding knowingly to serious runners. Feeling the soothing ache in my muscles after an hour.

Exercise has always helped me focus, and now, without it, I don't know what to do. I want to leave here, leave my body, and feel the fresh air on my face.

I feel like a lion trapped in a cage.

Gabriel has just left for work.

Lucky climbs slowly up the stairs in our house and saunters over to our room. Without a second of hesitation, he climbs into our unmade bed. He turns around to get comfortable, then curls up into a ball huddled amid the piles of covers.

I swear that mutt is mocking me.

GABRIEL

"Salomé, come back here this instant! This won't turn out well for you if I have to come get you!"

The mother sighs, clearly at the end of her rope. A little girl of about three walks past the bench Gabriel is sitting on. Two blonde pigtails bob up and down to the rhythm of her tiny sandal-clad feet, moving fast to keep from getting caught.

"Do you hear me, Salomé? I won't bring you to play on the slide anymore . . ."

The young brunette leaves her stroller just long enough to grab her daughter by the arm. The girl whines, visibly unhappy to be leaving. The two figures move away from the playground.

"Have you been waiting long?" Emma asks as she sits down on the bench. She puts down the black bag she's always carrying and greets Gabriel with friendly kisses on both cheeks.

"No, I don't think so. I've gotten used to being alone, you know. I often sit here and watch the kids play. I find it soothing."

"You think screaming kids are soothing?" jokes Emma.

Gabriel doesn't answer. He likes watching children play, yell, fall, get up, and climb around without ever taking a breather. Other people's children.

The idea of having his own child to play with on the slide, push on the swings, and comfort after a fall disappeared when Chloé died. He waited patiently for years for his wife to share his desire to have kids. Without becoming bitter or resentful. He knew it took two to make a baby, and since he loved Chloé more than anything, he could wait. He was patient. He was confident in their future.

But now . . . Look where that's gotten him.

The caterer he'd hired for his wife's thirtieth birthday knocked on his door yesterday afternoon and left Gabriel with a full buffet for forty people. He'd paid the balance on everything at the beginning of the year, and though he had let the guests know and canceled the DJ a month ago, he had totally forgotten about the caterer. The mountains of smoked salmon, sliced roast beef, pasta salad with scallops, tabbouleh, and more were intimidating. He put a tiny part of it in his freezer, then took some to his parents—his father would be thrilled to eat the same thing all week.

Then he called Geoffrey, but he was off on a weekend getaway with some recent conquest he'd probably met on a dating site.

He turned to Lucky, but he was no help.

So he called Emma and invited her to hang out with him for the evening. The young woman explained that she hadn't eaten a thing all day because she'd been following a troupe of girls around, shooting a never-ending bachelorette party: brunch, followed by a scavenger hunt through the city, lap-dance lessons, cocktail-making lessons, and spa treatments in the late afternoon—none of which Emma actually got to enjoy, of course. Gabriel laughed at Emma's description of her day as a rented photojournalist, and told her that she was in luck because he had enough food to feed an army. Emma didn't ask any questions about where the gargantuan amounts of food had come from. That's one of the things he likes about her: her tact.

They've seen each other several times since she came over to help him choose pictures of Chloé a little over a month ago, and much to Gabriel's surprise—he's always been reserved and even shy—he's come to consider Emma a friend. A confidante, even. He's shown her his favorite places in and around Saint-Malo: the rock sculptures in Rothéneuf, the fort on Petit Bé Island just off the coast, the ramparts and their amazing view of the port. Emma followed him to each site as if she were seeing the places for the first time. She didn't tell him that she had already photographed every inch of the city for the tourism office.

Emma takes a few spontaneous shots of children on the merry-go-round. Click, click. She freezes their movement on camera.

"So, what do you want to do?"

"I thought I'd take you out for some crêpes in the best crêperie in the city."

"Simple as that, huh?"

"Simple as that," answers Gabriel with a smile.

EMMA

Am I falling in love with Gabriel? I have no idea. I'm not even sure I really want to ask myself the question.

Do I like him? Of course. We understand one another, and have since the beginning. Everything's easy. It's like we were made to get along, like we've been *reunited*. We have similar taste and the same sense of humor. He likes the simple things in life, and I'm hardly complicated. I love to decide things last minute and he's all for the unpredictable. He could be a great friend—my best friend, even.

Do I find him attractive? He's definitely handsome. Especially since he doesn't seem to realize it and makes no effort at all to be seductive. And his vulnerability is touching, it's true . . . He sometimes makes me think of the sparrows that used to accidentally bang into the sliding glass door at my parents' house. I would gently pick up their unconscious bodies and carefully place them in old shoe boxes lined with cotton balls. Then I'd watch over them until they started to stir, until they worked up enough strength to fly away again. I know Gabriel won't stay in the box for long. He's been seriously injured, it's true, but his will to live is strong.

Am I getting attached to him? More than I intended when I decided to move here for just a few months.

Does this mean my plans are history? Not at all. Our "relationship" will only last a few months anyway, then I'll leave this country forever. I need broader horizons to fulfil my dreams.

As for him, I have no idea how he feels about me or what he expects of me, of us. I don't feel like a buoy he's simply using to get through the mourning period. I think I'm more than that. He likes spending time with me, though I've noticed that he freezes up from time to time, probably overwhelmed by a memory that suddenly surfaces. I almost never talk about his wife, and he mentions her only rarely outside of the group therapy sessions.

We take long walks with Lucky, go out for dinner, and study all the different species of crabs at the market together, fascinated but feigning disgust as they writhe on the tables. We sit on the sandy beach amid the hordes of tourists and entertain ourselves by imagining what their lives are like.

"The lady in the fuchsia bathing suit won't go into the water with her husband because she's never worked up the courage to tell him she doesn't know how to swim," I muse.

"Or maybe she just doesn't like the cold water. She's always dreamed of spending their summer vacation on the Mediterranean coast, but since his parents live in Saint-Malo, he won't even entertain the idea of going anywhere else," Gabriel counters.

"Or maybe they partied all night long. She danced until dawn, drinking glass after glass of champagne, and now she has a terrible hangover."

"Could be. That would explain the sunglasses. Oh wait, maybe that's just because it's sunny . . ."

"Honestly, that seems much less likely!" I tease, an overly skeptical look on my face.

Gabriel laughs and throws his hands up in defeat. Then he starts eagerly hunting through the crowd to find a new subject for our little game. I watch him out of the corner of my eye, thrilled to see him behaving so lightheartedly.

I know having me around lessens his load, that I'm helping him make his way back to the light, but he's still bogged down in memories and nostalgia. I know I can't rush him; we have to take things a day at a time. I know I can't *save* him. All I can do is be there for him and support him, without getting preoccupied by my own growing feelings.

Today he's accompanying me to the wedding I have to photograph. He didn't have anything planned for the weekend, and when I jokingly asked him to come, he jumped at the chance. I've lent him my spare camera and given him a crash course on framing. When I introduce him to the couple as my intern, nobody seems the least bit surprised.

We both follow the bride as she gets ready with her bridesmaids, and I explain to Gabriel in a whisper that the most important thing is to be so unobtrusive that they forget you're there, so you can get the most spontaneous pictures possible. It's not about taking as many photos as you can in the hope of getting one or two good ones, but about discreetly capturing the *right* moment.

The bride comes down the stairs of her family's home to her eager groom, waiting for her in a white suit on the porch. I take a few pictures as they kiss. Gabriel stands next to me, motionless.

"Why aren't you shooting?"

"Shooting what? The couple posing with stiff smiles? The clearly premeditated kiss?" Gabriel asks with a bewildered look. He doesn't understand that these conventional poses are exactly what my clients hire me to capture.

After that it's the usual ceremonies, first civil, then religious. The signing of the official ledger at the town hall, then the grand exit from the little Breton church under a cloud of bubbles instead of the frankly less agreeable, more traditional handfuls of rice. During the cocktail reception, with Gabriel right behind me, I try to take portraits of each guest, as well as a giant group photo. There are at least two hundred guests, and corralling all of them is a real challenge. I somehow manage to climb up the wall that surrounds the private garden where the festivities are being held, because I have to take the picture from above to get everyone in the frame. I give Gabriel the thankless task of getting them to pose together on the grass below, with the young newlyweds in the middle obviously. He enthusiastically heads off to let each of the little groups—all of them chatting with a glass of champagne in hand—know what we need from them. In less than ten minutes, he's succeeded in getting all two hundred people into the frame for the photo I want to take.

I'm impressed. I give him a thumbs-up, and he just raises an eyebrow as if to say, "That wasn't so hard!"

"Hands up, everyone. Ready, one, two, threeee!"

Glad that's done. The guests immediately head off toward the hors d'oeuvre table. The experience seems to have left them famished.

Gabriel holds out his hand to help me down from the wall without damaging my camera. When my palm meets his, I feel butterflies in my stomach.

CHAPTER 8
SEPTEMBER 2013

CHLOÉ

Gabriel seems to be doing better. He's stopped crying and playing depressing music on repeat, and he doesn't spend hours sitting on the couch anymore. The change took time, but the results are there. He's not *lost* anymore.

Could he have already forgotten me? Could he possibly have gotten over the loss of the woman he shared his life with for eight years in just four months?

He's always out all weekend and often comes home late during the week. Sometimes he even *sings* in the shower in the morning. Even the dog seems surprised. Could Gabriel be thinking about someone other than me? Has he confused getting on with his life with moving on to the next thing?

I refuse to believe that the photographer woman who sometimes comes by the house is behind this change. She can't be my rival. She doesn't look anything like me.

First of all, she's a tomboy. Short mannish hair. Zero makeup: no eyeshadow, no lipstick. If I were her, I wouldn't dare leave the house.

Two big blue eyes dominate her face. They're disproportionately large and make her look a bit like a manga heroine.

She's thin, skinny even. No chest. Her hips are her only redeeming quality, but they're nothing to write home about.

As for her clothes, from what I've seen, she has a lot to learn. You don't seduce a man dressed in an old pair of denim Converse.

With her camera around her neck every minute of every day, she seems to really believe she's the reincarnation of Doisneau or something. I say Doisneau because he's the only photographer who comes to mind. Come to think of it, there aren't many famous photographers, are there?

It's weird that she's never thought to participate in a makeover show.

Okay, fine, she gets Gabriel to *laugh*. Isn't she amazing. She distracts him, takes his mind off things. But there's no reason to imagine anything more. No. Impossible! I would be hurt.

Nonetheless, something is going on.

I hear Gabriel whistling as he vacuums. It's time to do something. To do what anyone would do in my shoes.

Move objects and turn on the CD player in the middle of the night . . . Anything to keep my memory near and dear to my husband's heart.

GABRIEL

Emma wants to be more than friends, he can tell. Maybe he's known since the beginning, but it's just easier to keep pretending.

He sees her looking at him a bit too intently, her shy smiles, the expectation behind the sentences she doesn't always finish. He doesn't know what to think about it, but he's beginning to realize he needs to be honest with himself. And with her.

He finds Emma attractive, of course. Physically she's nothing like Chloé, but she's the kind of fragile girl that you want to protect, despite her façade of self-confidence. He knows he could take her in his arms like an abandoned kitten. She acts strong and rebellious, claims she wants to see the world and that nothing is tying her down, but he can see the chink in her armor.

Does he want to break through her shell?

Yes, he's drawn to Emma. Her gamine physique is incredibly alluring. Her big, innocent blue eyes, her boyish pixie cut, the way she wrinkles her nose and pouts when she's annoyed. It all brings back a strangely familiar tingling, but he refuses to dwell on it. Gabriel is not the kind of guy who cheats on his wife. Even if she's dead. And Chloé was not the kind of woman who could accept being replaced so quickly. She certainly wouldn't approve if she could see what's been going on the past few months.

And yet . . . Before Emma came into his life, he was dying, slowly but surely. That much is clear. He had no goals, no desires; he simply sat back and watched the hours of the day go by. Emma's carefree eagerness and her ability to look at everything with wonderment are good for him.

The front door rings and Lucky stands up with a bark. Gabriel finds the mailman on his porch.

"A delivery for you. Sign here, please," says the postal worker without so much as a glance at Gabriel. The man has just started his route and doesn't have a second to lose on small talk. Gabriel quickly signs on the screen of the little black machine the mailman is holding out, then takes his package.

In the living room, he opens the bubble envelope to find the latest novel by Amélie Nothomb. A black-and-white photo of the author on the back, and on the front, her name written in bubblegum pink. He didn't order this book. Intrigued, he unfolds the invoice to see it's addressed to Chloé. She must have preordered it on the Internet to be sure she got it as soon as it was published.

Gabriel fans through the crisp pages, savoring the smell of freshly printed ink. Chloé will never read this new book by her favorite author. The novelist comes out with a book every year with a regularity that doesn't fit Gabriel's idea of what an author should be, but Chloé had made it an annual tradition to read each new volume in a single night, in the bathtub. It had become a kind of ritual.

All of a sudden, Gabriel feels morose. Sadness and nostalgia wash over him in crushing waves. He doesn't bother to fight it.

He hates baths—and Amélie Nothomb. He's always thought her novels are little more than a series of variations on the same story. The novelist has found the mother lode of themes, and while he feels she's right to exploit it, he doesn't understand why her readers haven't figured it out yet.

Chloé, of course, had been of a different mind. She had L-O-V-E loved almost all her books. Whenever her favorite author was doing a signing at a bookstore, Chloé put it in her calendar—even if that meant canceling appointments or taking a day off. Once, a few years ago, Gabriel went with her to meet her idol at the Virgin Megastore on the Champs-Elysées. He hadn't expected to see so many fans waiting happily in line for a few hasty scribbles. Chloé got more and more excited as they neared the novelist. Gabriel mostly remembers how much his feet hurt from standing around.

"You don't have to wait in line with me, you know. We can meet up in a café later if you want."

"No, I'm happy to stay. I just hope the wait will be worth it," Gabriel sighed.

When they finally reached the table where Amélie Nothomb was signing books like an assembly-line machine, the author took the copy of *Tokyo Fiancée* that Chloé shyly held out and asked, "Who should I make this one out to?" without looking up.

Her awestruck admirer mumbled, "Chloé," and hurriedly opened the front cover when the novel was handed back to her to see the sought-after autograph: *For Chloé,* followed by a signature that vaguely resembled an intertwined *A* and *N*.

A redhead behind them in the line sighed loudly and nudged Gabriel to move, so Chloé slipped the book into her purse.

But Gabriel didn't budge. He stopped in front of the novelist, who was waiting for the next book to sign. "That's it?" he demanded. "We waited hours for that? My girlfriend knows almost all your books by heart, and all she gets is the same chicken scratch you scrawl on every copy in less time than it takes to say your name out loud?"

He was suddenly furious for Chloé, disappointed for her, despite the fact that she was thrilled just to have had the chance to walk past her favorite author. When Chloé pulled on his sleeve, embarrassed to see him act that way, he obediently fell in behind her, but not without glaring at the burly security guard who had quickly made his way to the scene.

"Please forgive him, he doesn't know what he's saying . . . Thank you so much for the autograph," Chloé mumbled with a smile and a kind of bow to the surprised writer.

"Next year I'll come alone," she said once they were outside. "You were so rude! And if there's an author who cares about her readers, it's her! I don't even know why I brought you . . ."

After they'd walked in silence for several minutes, Chloé finally smiled at Gabriel, a knowing look in her eyes, and continued in a different tone, "I can't take you anywhere! But I'm sure she'll remember me, thanks to you. Maybe her next protagonist will even be named Chloé—who knows!"

Gabriel sighs, remembering the scene. How many novels will Chloé miss out on? How many would she have devoured if her life hadn't been so suddenly and unfairly taken from her?

He stands up, novel in hand, and climbs the stairs to the bathroom. He plugs the drain and runs the hot water. He takes his shirt off without undoing the buttons and pulls down his jeans and boxers. He steps into the bathtub, lies down, and puts his head under the water. Everything goes quiet. He stays there until his lungs can't take it anymore.

Wiping his hands on the towel sitting next to the sink, he grabs the book. He gets comfortable and starts reading to the soothing sound of running water slowly filling the tub.

EMMA

Everything is going too slowly. Sometimes I feel like Gabriel and I are on the same wavelength, but other times he seems so cold. He can be attentive one minute and distant the next, as if he's not even there.

Yesterday we were in the car together and everything was great. He was taking me home after a quick bite in a little brasserie, telling me what he likes about his job, trying really hard to convince me that it isn't as boring and tedious as people think. I absentmindedly pushed the power button on the stereo and a CD started playing. "Send Me an Angel" by Scorpions filled the inside of the car.

Gabriel stopped talking midsentence, as if he'd lost track of his thoughts.

"Are you okay?" I asked.

He stayed silent. After a few seemingly endless seconds of me trying to figure out what I could possibly have said that was out of line, he turned off the music. He didn't say a single word the whole rest of the drive. Just a terse, "Good night, Emma," when we got back to my apartment.

I just don't get it.

I want to live my life in the fast lane. I don't have time to wait for someone who takes one step forward and three steps back.

This month the group is talking about guilt. Each of the participants was asked to make a list of the things that make him or her feel guilty. Edith is trying to help them with those feelings, to lighten their load.

Oscar talks for a long time. His mother committed suicide when he was sixteen. She'd been depressed for several years, but nobody had noticed that she was getting worse. In the end, she swallowed several bottles of sleeping pills and anxiety drugs, and Oscar was the one who found her body when he came home from school. He explains that he's racked with guilt, yet knows that blaming himself for the past four years has kept him from moving on.

"I'm mad at myself for not noticing . . . Or, really, for noticing and not doing anything out of habit. I feel like I never knew my mother any other way. She was always apathetic like that. I never saw her get excited about anything, and I thought that was normal . . . I'm mad at myself for not coming home earlier that day, for not being able to bring her back. I blame myself for not being enough, for not making her happy, for not being a good enough son, for not being able to make her want to stay here with me . . ."

The air in the room is heavy when Oscar stops talking. His quiet sniffling, which he's clearly trying to stop, is the only sound to be heard. I can tell he's really opened up. He's let out all the pent-up emotions he'd never shared with anyone until tonight.

"I blame myself for not being there when Chloé drowned," says Gabriel softly, almost inaudibly. "I wasn't with her when she died. I don't know if she was scared, if she was surprised, if she was in pain. I don't know any of that because I wasn't there. Of course, it's no use dwelling on it. It's not going to get me through this. But my wife is dead and she was all alone. That's what haunts me. Every single day. That she was all alone, that nobody was there to help her, to save her . . ."

The others nod. They all understand his feelings of powerlessness. Marie-Hélène, who'd left the hospital for just half an hour: "Sacha didn't wait for me. He died before I could hold him one last time." Laura, who regrets letting her husband buy a motorcycle though there's nothing she could have done. Gisèle, who found out over the phone while she was in line at the grocery store that her husband had had a fatal heart attack: "I actually took the time to pay for everything. It was too late anyway . . ."

One step forward, three steps back.

CHAPTER 9
OCTOBER 2013

CHLOÉ

Fall is just around the corner and I'm standing still. Gabriel is moving on, and I'm stuck here. "For better or for worse," he said once.

But only "until death do us part," I suppose . . .

Memories of our wedding are running through my head. The months of preparations for the big day. I'd wanted everything to be perfect. I'd planned the most beautiful ceremony, something so stunning our guests would remember it as the best wedding they had ever attended. I had dreamed of it since I was a little girl, wrapped in a white sheet for a dress . . .

Gabriel simply went with it. It wasn't his dream, but since it was mine, it was just as important to him. If we had done it his way, we would have gotten married at the town hall and had a barbecue in his mother's backyard.

I chose "Starry Night" to be our theme, and Gabriel spent hours cutting stars out of construction paper, painting them gold, then adding glitter with a paint brush. On our wedding day, he had to admit that the result was magnificent: I had covered the ceiling with dark-blue fabric and glued the sparkling stars to it one by one. For the place cards, he had even agreed to make more than one hundred and fifty origami stars, on which I then carefully wrote the names of each of our guests in gold pen. We spent a lot of evenings together, side by side, working on the decorations for our wedding.

I'd hired the best caterer in the Paris metro area and selected the most expensive champagne and wines. I begged Gabriel to let us have gospel singers at the church and worked on him for days about renting a castle with extensive grounds—making sure to highlight the fact that I'd let my dream of a pond go as proof of how reasonable I could be. In the end, he always gave in, even though he wasn't thrilled about having to go into debt to pay for most of the wedding.

"Don't you think it would be smarter to have a smaller wedding and use our savings for a down payment on a house in a few months?" Gabriel tried.

I hated when he sounded like a banker.

"I'm not one of your clients, sweetheart. This wedding is all I've ever dreamed of and I want it to be stunning. I want us to remember it for the rest of our lives . . ."

I made pleading Puss-in-Boots eyes, and Gabriel couldn't resist.

I controlled everything, down to the tiniest detail. There was no room for improvisation and even less for mistakes. I chose the texts for the religious ceremony and checked the speeches the best man and maid of honor were going to give, because while I was fairly sure that Oriane would come up with something acceptable, I didn't have much faith in Geoffrey. I tasted all the dishes that would be served, made a list of songs for the DJ to play in a precise order. I even chose the plastic cake topper of a bride and groom myself at a specialized boutique and got all the thank-you cards ready before the wedding took place. I didn't leave a single thing to chance.

Gabriel didn't understand why I was so frenzied, but decided that if it made me happy, that's what mattered. He knew that spontaneity wasn't my strong suit. I liked to think ahead, plan, and control every situation.

When the big day arrived, it was perfect. Not a single incident. By four in the morning, we were the only ones left. Our guests had gone home, exhausted. The DJ had packed up his equipment and offered his best wishes for a happy marriage before taking off in his van. Gabriel and I sat outside on the grounds of the castle, under the starry night sky.

"Wait here, okay? I'll be right back," Gabriel said as he ran off.

He reappeared a few minutes later and sat down next to me. He held something that looked like a tiny hot-air balloon.

"What's that?"

"Our very own firefly. We're going to make a wish and watch it fly away. I thought it went pretty well with the 'Starry Night' theme . . ."

At that exact moment, I wanted to cry. Instead, I leaned over and rested my head on my husband's shoulder.

We lit the burner together and the paper balloon inflated from the heat. The "firefly" rose slowly into the sky, and we watched the spot of light until it disappeared. I think it was the most touching moment of our whole wedding.

The only one I hadn't planned.

It's seven o'clock in the morning. The alarm clock goes off in our bedroom.

I watch as Gabriel gets up, his eyes still heavy with sleep. He walks, only half awake, to the bathroom to take a shower. He yawns as he turns on the faucet. The spray of hot water hits him square in the chest. He reaches out to grab his shampoo from the edge of the bathtub and accidentally knocks over two bottles of glitter paint. Bright yellow and dark blue.

He picks one up, confused. Now he's awake.

I smile.

Hello, sweetheart. I'm still here.

GABRIEL

For the past few days he's been feeling almost harassed by his wife, or rather, by memories of his wife that keep fighting their way to the surface at the most unlikely moments. A song that they both liked starts playing at the grocery store while he's shopping. A little note she scrawled on a Post-it turns up in a kitchen drawer.

Just yesterday the television screen turned to static, so he had to move the entertainment unit to check the cable wires. After three minutes of shoving with all his might, he finally managed to move the thing a few inches and found an earring on the floor. A small silver feather Chloé had spent weeks looking for.

He wants to scream. *Leave me alone, Chloé!* As if she were somehow responsible for these painful everyday coincidences. Part of him believes it's his guilt messing with him.

Because Emma kissed him two days ago. Or maybe he started it?

They were walking in silence along the levee after a nice dinner out. He wishes he could say he'd had too much to drink, but that would be a lie.

All of a sudden, she stopped and he turned around to see why. Her blue eyes staring right at him, she waited.

A silent ultimatum.

She wouldn't stop staring, and he stared back.

He moved in closer. Took her face in his hands and stroked her hair.

Yes, he had kissed her. Innocently at first. His lips brushed shyly across hers. Emma stood on her tiptoes and grabbed hold of his collar. She pulled Gabriel in closer, still staring.

The second kiss was anything but hesitant.

When they finally caught their breath, Emma looked at him inquisitively. He hugged her tight without a word.

Ever since, he hasn't been able to stop thinking about Chloé. And Emma too.

He's lost. He's racked with guilt, but can't keep his heart from skipping a beat when he thinks about the kiss. He wants to call Emma, but hangs up before he finishes dialing her cell number.

He woke up at dawn this morning and has been daydreaming under the covers, waiting for the alarm to go off. He notices the book sitting on Chloé's nightstand. One of the few things he hasn't put away yet. *A Secret Kept* by Tatiana de Rosnay. He reaches out to pick it up and read the back cover.

Chloé was three-quarters of the way through, if the piece of folded paper she was using as a bookmark is any indication. As he flips distractedly through the book, he accidentally drops the small piece of ivory paper. He picks it up and unfolds it, more out of instinct than curiosity.

A few words, jotted down in blue ink.

I'm glad you came back.

Without you I felt so dark.

I thought I had lost you.

Without you I felt so blue.

It's not Chloé's handwriting. It doesn't even look like a woman's handwriting. Gabriel only knows one person who writes lyrics in middle-school-level English. Just one loser who cobbles together two chords on an acoustic guitar while mumbling ridiculous lines to the only sickly sweet melody he knows. Just one loser who thinks that looking a bit like a rock star will get him all the ladies.

And that loser's name is Simon.

It doesn't seem like he has too much trouble attaining his goals, however. And the musical attempts Gabriel finds appallingly bad somehow usually manage to attract women.

Chloé in particular.

Gabriel clenches his teeth, crumples the paper into a little ball, and throws it across the room. He's not mad, he's relieved.

He picks up his phone and dials Emma's number.

This time, he doesn't hang up.

EMMA

After we kissed, I was sure that Gabriel would never call me back. That I had been too forward, too impatient.

But my phone did finally ring, and I feel like something has finally changed. Gabriel is ready to move on—with me by his side.

Just as I was about to give up on us, we started to get serious.

We don't go out so much anymore. Frankly, I've seen everything interesting Saint-Malo has to offer. He took a few days off work, and we spent almost an entire week holed up at his place.

We made love in every room in his house. Except the bedroom; that door always stays closed. We took over the little guest room and the rather rough fold-out couch after giving the living-room couch, kitchen counter, chest freezer in the garage, stairs—too hard—and bathtub a go.

Those few days away from the rest of the world were an amazing break. We learned things about each other, got to know one another. Everything seems so simple with him.

I know, what a cliché, right?

I was patient and supportive, and the sparrow has finally ventured outside the box. Gabriel is no longer a fragile little creature in need of empathy and compassion.

Not in the least.

Now when I feel his arms around me, his breath on my skin, I'm the one who feels small. When he looks at me, all I can see in his eyes is his desire to be right where he is, with me, here and now.

After a few days he had to return to work. We had to come back to the real world. Ever since, time away from him seems to pass so slowly it's like torture. I've never felt anything like it. I love the sensation, the excitement. But I hate it too—I hardly recognize myself anymore. I'm constantly checking my phone to make sure I haven't accidentally turned off the ringer or missed a text from Gabriel. When I'm with him, I try to act like nothing's changed, but this is the first time I've experienced what it's like to love someone so much and be so happy it hurts.

Of course, I never planned to actually fall in love with him. It really complicates the decisions I've made to make my dreams come true, but I'm trying not to think about that right now. I still plan on taking off early next year, but between now and then so much could happen . . . Who knows, maybe he'll want to leave everything behind and follow me to the ends of the earth? That's not so crazy, is it?

I haven't told him about my plans yet. He thinks that being a "war photographer," as he puts it, is a vague dream, the kind that never becomes a reality. I didn't want to tell him otherwise in the beginning, and now I feel like it's too late. We've just started a life together, and I can't imagine telling him that I intend to leave the country in a few months. When we met, I did tell him that my stay in Saint-Malo was temporary, that I was looking to save some money before heading off on my adventure. But apparently he either didn't believe me or forgot the conversation. Or maybe he thinks our relationship will change everything.

In some ways, he's right.

For now I'm simply enjoying life. I'm enjoying his affection, his gentleness, his kindness. I'm starting to really care for him, and I'd rather not think about what comes next. He's already lost his wife; I don't want to be the second woman to abandon him in just a few months . . .

I hope that, when the time comes, he won't hate me. I hope he'll understand, that he'll be able to forgive me.

CHAPTER 10
NOVEMBER 2013

CHLOÉ

I watch as Gabriel sits in a café near the city ramparts with his new conquest.

I decided I didn't want to see—and especially hear—any more of what has been going on at our house over the past few days. Everything suddenly started going so fast, and that tramp basically moved in as I watched, powerless to stop her.

I'm furious. If I could rip her big, innocent eyes right out of her head, I would. And I would enjoy it. I'd make them jump out of their sockets with a dessert spoon: pop, pop. And I'd shove her stupid camera down her throat. Click, click.

I'm not mad at Gabriel. Well, not too mad. He's lost and in need of affection, nothing more. He's not wearing his wedding ring anymore, but he never liked wearing it anyway. That doesn't mean anything.

As for her . . . I'm sure that bitch thinks she's actually in love with him, that it's for real. I'm sure she's already started imagining herself as the next Mrs. Hamon. She's even co-opted the dog. She won him over with belly rubs and treats.

The waiter comes over. Gabriel orders a Coke and she asks for an Earl Grey tea. Earl Grey tea! Is there any duller, more boring drink on the planet? Why not a cup of chamomile while you're at it, Little Miss Husband Stealer?

I watch as they fawn over each other, kissing and stroking like two teenagers cut off from the rest of the world. They're shameless.

It's unbearable.

The waiter comes back with a tray. He puts a Coke down in front of Gabriel and a violet lemonade in front of *her*. I don't even know her name.

She looks up with the surprised expression that never seems to leave her face and tells the waiter it's not what she ordered.

"Are you sure?" he asks with a frown. "I wrote down 'a Coke and a violet lemonade.'"

"No. No, I'm sure I said Earl Grey tea!"

She's bewildered by the situation, but it's okay. Lemonade will be fine, nothing to fuss about. Great, she's nice too. She doesn't want to put anyone out.

The annoyed waiter takes the glass back to the bar anyway.

Gabriel is as white as a sheet.

Violet lemonade is my favorite drink.

GABRIEL

He can't reach Simon. Ever since he found the note in Chloé's book, Gabriel has been trying to call him, but he keeps getting his machine. "Hi, this is Simon. Leave me a message and *maybe* I'll call you back!" Gabriel lets out a disdainful snort every time he hears it.

He's not really mad, but he needs to know the truth. Was his wife cheating on him? He can't believe it: Chloé wasn't a deceitful person, and he'd seen the guilt she'd carried for months after ending her friend-ship with Simon. And he couldn't have been so blind as to have stood by without noticing his wife having an affair with this guy, right?

Gabriel has been going over this for weeks now, and he still has too many questions. He's decided to let it go. Simon doesn't answer his phone or call back, and maybe it's for the best. What would knowing change anyway? He doesn't want to tarnish the memory of his wife.

Better to live in the present. And Emma is the present, not Chloé.

When he's with her, he feels alive again. She makes him forget about everything else. The beginning of a relationship is always magi-cal like that. He wants to surrender to it. She brings color to his world, which has been nothing but black and white for six months. Six months already . . .

Yes, he really cares about Emma. But deep down he knows that if he could choose, it's Chloé he would want back by his side.

Because the grief is still suffocating sometimes, more than he can bear. Her voice, her face, her smell. It all comes back to him in flashes at the most unexpected times. Though it only lasts a few seconds, the pain is overwhelming, like having a knife plunged into his heart or having the air knocked out of him so hard he falls to his knees. A kind of Chloé shock. Her hand in his, her hair flowing over the pillowcase, the way she danced with her MP3 player cranked all the way up in the middle of the silent living room.

Sometimes he can admit to himself that his memories must be idealized versions of reality, brighter than the original, the emotions more intense. "Be careful not to deify the person you've lost," Edith keeps repeating.

But when the memories invade his brain of their own volition, he has zero perspective. He misses Chloé; he misses everything about her. He feels torn, almost schizophrenic.

When he opens his front door to take Lucky for a walk—the poor dog has been pacing the house for an hour now—Gabriel comes face-to-face with Elise, the receptionist from the gym where his wife worked. She shuffles her weight from one foot to the other and finally awkwardly hands over a small box.

"Hello . . . I know it's taken me awhile, but here are the things Chloé left in her locker. It was padlocked, and since we didn't need it, we didn't do anything about it. But now that we've hired a new trainer, we need to make space for her, so . . . I didn't throw anything out, I just put it all in the box. I thought it was your place to go through it, that maybe you'd find something you'd want to keep . . ."

The poor woman is so uncomfortable that she would literally run away if she could. Gabriel thanks her and lets her know she can go. Relieved, she says good-bye and heads back to her car, parked up the street.

Gabriel puts the box on the floor in the corner of the living room. He wishes he could just throw it all away, because he's already haunted by memories. But he knows he won't.

Inside the box, he finds sports bras, a neon-pink tank top, and a pair of black minishorts. Part of Chloé's job was to look hot when she taught her classes. "We have to make our customers want to come back somehow, sweetheart!" An expired tube of cream for easing muscle soreness. A bath towel and an all-in-one shower gel and shampoo.

And at the very bottom, a big white envelope. *Saint-Malo Hospital.*

He opens it. There's a stack of papers stapled together. Gabriel reads the words typed on the pages, but they don't make any sense.

```
Post-operative report

Surgical termination of pregnancy at
patient's request.

Pre-operative meds: Rohypnol + Ibuprofen
```

```
Local anesthesia: four shots of Xylocaine

Dilation of cervix

Aspiration

Conclusion:    Pregnancy    successfully
terminated at nine weeks gestation.
```

He looks for the date. *January 2013.*

His head starts spinning. He can't hold back the caustic bile that's building up in his throat.

EMMA

After a week of zero contact, Gabriel finally showed up at my apartment this morning before work. When I saw that the wall clock across from my fold-out bed read a quarter to eight, I almost didn't get up to answer the intercom.

But it just kept ringing and ringing, so I decided to crawl out from under the covers, cursing the thoughtless person who was waking me at such an ungodly hour.

"It's me!"

I kept quiet.

"It's Gabriel. Will you open the door?"

"You think you can just disappear and then show up unannounced whenever you want? That I'm at your beck and call?"

As soon as the words leave my mouth, I regret it. I can't help it, though. I want to move forward and I'm tired of getting bogged down in Gabriel's past.

I push the button to open the downstairs door. A few minutes later, Gabriel comes into the apartment. He closes the door gently behind himself and remains in the entryway, his arms hanging down at his sides, like a kid who knows he's in trouble.

I'm moved by his sad face.

"Want some coffee?"

"Sure, if you're making some for yourself too."

I take out a capsule and put it into the machine. The hot black liquid streams into the cup.

Gabriel sits on one of the two bar stools. I turn my back to him.

"Are you okay? What was so urgent that you needed to tell me at this time of day? It's been almost a week since I've heard from you! I left you messages, sent you texts . . . I was starting to worry. Thinking that you regretted it all, that you didn't want to see me anymore but weren't brave enough to tell me to my face."

"No, it's not that at all . . ."

Gabriel stares at the steam coming out of the coffee cup.

"What is it then? Tell me!"

He looks up and bites his bottom lip, a pensive expression on his face.

"I've been thinking a lot over the past few days. I wanted to take some time . . . Everything has moved so fast between us, and I wanted to be sure about what we're doing."

I don't like the direction this is headed. He's about to tell me it's too soon for him, that he feels like he's cheating on his wife, that he's not ready to be in a new relationship . . . I grip my coffee cup. All this, for nothing.

"I want you to move in with me."

I'm stunned. I can't move.

Gabriel stands up and comes around the table to stand right in front of me. With one hand he gently pushes my chin upward until I'm gazing into his eyes.

"If you think it's too soon, tell me. But you already spend so many nights at my house, and I don't think you're especially fond of your studio since you've only had it for six months. Plus, Lucky adores you, even if, obviously, you're not moving in for him . . . Anyway, if you'd rather wait, I und—"

I place my index finger on Gabriel's mouth to shush him. I wait a few seconds, then touch my lips to his. I run my hands through his curly hair and pull him close. We kiss for a long time, his arms wrapped around me.

When I step back, he takes a deep breath.

"I'll take that as a yes?"

CHAPTER 11
DECEMBER 2013

CHLOÉ

Everybody is getting ready for the holidays.

Everybody except me, of course.

My rival has moved into the house. I watched, powerlessly, as she brought over a couple of boxes and a suitcase. She didn't have much—she could have been living in the streets before for all I know.

I realize I'm being mean. I hate being like this, but I can't help it anymore. The worst part is that everything that's happening is my fault. I can't even be mad at Gabriel for wanting to get on with his life.

She's put her things away in my closet. They moved the fold-out couch in the guest room so that now it's on the wall facing the door. She must be into feng shui, or maybe it's just her way of making herself at home. As if sleeping with *my* husband in *my* house weren't enough. At least they've had the decency not to move into our bedroom.

She put her toothbrush next to Gabriel's in the cup on the bathroom sink. Isn't that cute.

She's filled up the kitchen cabinets with her Earl Grey tea bags and put a bright-red coffee maker in the middle of the counter. Gabriel even cleared a shelf of the bookcase in the living room so she'd have a place to put her camera and all her other crap. He came across a picture of me while he was doing it, but he hardly seemed to notice. I think I could make all the doors slam and shatter all the windows one by one without him batting an eye. He's even taken off the chain he wore around his neck with my wedding ring on it. He put it away in a forgotten corner somewhere.

It looks like I've lost.

What else can I possibly do to keep him from forgetting about me? Was I wrong about him? Maybe he didn't really love me that much after all.

They went out to buy a Christmas tree this morning, then spent an hour decorating it together, taking out the ornaments we had so carefully organized in an old moving box, one by one. Gabriel and I always used to choose one new ornament at a different Christmas market each year: Strasbourg, Brussels, Cologne. We took a weekend trip to visit a different one every winter. We sipped mulled wine to distract us from our frozen fingers, enjoyed temporary ice-skating rinks, and rode Ferris wheels to get a glimpse of the cute wooden houses from above. We lovingly selected the prettiest ornament we could find and took it home with us, pleased with the success of our little getaway. A gilded drum, a blown-glass bulb, a white wicker snowman.

Gabriel hands the big carved wooden star to his new sweetheart and together they top the tall tree.

I scream out in pain, despite myself. I just need the release—it's not like either of them can hear me. They're in their perfect little bubble of happiness, while I . . . I don't even exist anymore.

Hell, I don't exist for *anyone* anymore.

I glare at my rival's calm, happy face. She looks like she's just hit the jackpot.

GABRIEL

Gabriel is lying in bed with Emma, absentmindedly playing with the charm necklace she's wearing. She grabs his hand and laughs. "You're tickling me!"

"Don't you ever take it off?"

"Just to shower. My great-grandmother gave it to me and it means a lot to me. If I lost it or broke it, I'd never be able to forgive myself."

Emma has been living with him for three weeks now, but he feels like it's been forever. He can't get over how quickly they clicked, how quickly their bond strengthened. She seems to know his taste for everything, from his favorite dessert to the TV shows he watches religiously. She knows exactly what shirt size and color to buy him. When she makes dinner, she whips up a chicken tagine, even though he's never told her it's his favorite dish. When he asks if she'd like to go to the movies, she suggests *The Wolf of Wall Street*, without having any idea that Gabriel is probably one of Martin Scorsese's biggest fans.

Over their eight years together, Chloé had never been able to remember that he hated chocolate ice cream and couldn't stand skinny jeans. Gabriel hates hearing the little voice in his head that loves to compare the two women, but he can't always quiet it. At first, Chloé was always better than Emma. Prettier, bolder, more feminine. But over the past few months, the tide seems to have turned. Emma is easier to get along with, a better listener, and funnier. Sometimes she's even sexier.

Emma's eyes are closed, but he knows she's not asleep yet. He's thinking about the conversation they had earlier tonight, following a phone call she had received. An international-aid NGO was looking for a photographer to report on the current situation in Gaza. A two-month mission that could lead to a permanent contract as a regional correspondent. Emma had sent her résumé and portfolio to all the NGOs and other organizations that might possibly be interested in hiring a photographer at the beginning of the year. Until now, she hadn't heard back.

When she'd hung up, she had jumped up and down with joy as she told Gabriel about the opportunity she was being offered. Not only would she be able to live her dream abroad, but she'd be paid for her photos!

He'd been dumbfounded. Sure, she had mentioned her plans before, but he had thought . . . What had he thought exactly? That a months-old relationship would make her forget about the dream she'd been working toward since she was a little girl? That she'd never get her big break and instead live out her days taking wedding photos of mind-numbingly ordinary couples every weekend?

He hid his feelings and gave her a congratulatory hug.

"When would you have to leave?"

"In just under two months, mid-February . . . But nothing's sure yet. I haven't said yes," Emma answered. She understood that Gabriel was hurt, though he hadn't said so. "And even if I do go, it'd only be for two months at first. It may not lead to anything . . ."

"You know you have to go, Emma. You said yourself that it's the chance of a lifetime. When you think about it, we hardly know each other."

"Why do you say that?"

"Because it's true! I adore you, but your dream is what counts, and that's as it should be. I don't want to be the one to hold you back," Gabriel said defeatedly, retreating without bothering to ask Emma how she felt about it all.

And now he can't get to sleep. He was just starting to feel safe again, and now everything is about to fall to pieces.

Should he try to keep Emma in Saint-Malo, knowing that he might have to watch her waste away at his side? Or should he do everything he can to help her realize her dreams?

EMMA

This should have been an amazing Christmas present, but it's put me in a difficult position. I've been waiting years for my big break, and now, when it finally happens, it's at the worst possible time.

I can't accept the job. I've gone over the offer a thousand times, but I just *can't*. It would be stupid to leave, now that I've moved in with Gabriel. I'm sure my dream can wait a few weeks or months more . . .

I haven't answered the HR guy who called me last Saturday. He gave me three weeks to think about it, because they know it's a big decision. You don't just pick up and leave behind everything you know in three days.

When I try to talk to Gabriel about it, he shuts down. He simply smiles and tells me I can't let a chance like this slip through my fingers. Hearing him repeat that over and over, I'm starting to think that maybe he's right. Maybe what we have isn't so special after all. Maybe he even regrets asking me to move in with him but is just too afraid to say so. Maybe this job offer is convenient for him . . .

As the days go by, I feel like he's becoming my adversary. We dance silently, step by step, in a fight with no words. I don't know what he's thinking, what he wants. Sometimes he seems so close, and then so far away again, as if I were already gone.

A single phone call has made it all start to crumble.

When I talk about the possibility of staying in Saint-Malo, he shakes his head sadly and says it would be stupid of me.

"But we're happy together, aren't we?"

"That's not the question, Emma. We're talking about *your* life, *your* dreams. My mother sacrificed her wants and needs to raise my brothers and me. She quit her job because my dad was always on business trips and there was no other way to make it work. But I know she loved being a florist. We grew up with her bitterness and regrets, despite the fact that she loved us and did her best to hide her listlessness. No, believe me, when you give up on the thing that makes you want to get out of bed every morning, you don't go unscathed. And neither do the people closest to you."

He stays on his high horse to avoid really talking about *us*.

At breakfast this morning, I finally decide to go for it.

"I'm not leaving."

He continues to stare out the window, coffee cup in hand.

"Yes, you are. You have to."

"I've made my decision and I'm not going to change my mind. So you can either keep being cold and distant, or you can take me in your arms and tell me what we're going to do for New Year's Eve."

Gabriel finally looks at me. He seems to be trying to decide whether or not I'm serious. He smiles—at last—though the sad gleam in his eyes hasn't disappeared altogether.

"Well, we have the choice between a wild party at Geoffrey's and a fancy dinner at my parents'. Let me elaborate a bit on our options, so you can make an informed decision. Plan A: meet my parents, who will study you like a lab rat, shine a bright light in your eyes, and put you through an interrogation worthy of the Inquisition to make sure you're not hiding some base and shameful secret. Other than that, they're great. Plan B: an eardrum-shattering experience with Geoffrey, who, after he's had a few drinks, will be unable to stop the litany of incredibly boring high school stories that inevitably pour from his mouth. He's great too but can't hold his liquor . . . I know that it's tough to decide, so think long and hard before you answer!"

CHAPTER 12
JANUARY 2014

CHLOÉ

When she so proudly announced that she wasn't leaving, I thought I was going to explode.

I thought everything was settled. Victory by forfeit, but victory nonetheless. As my mother would say, "Winning is all that matters."

I can still see my father and his hunched shoulders as he carried out the few boxes of stuff she was willing to let him take after the divorce. The little wave he'd given Oriane and me before getting into the same white Citroën he'd always driven. The forced smile he wore and the sad look in his eyes. Yes, his wife was leaving him, but more than that, he had to leave his daughters behind. The man who loved every minute he spent with us would have to make do with every other weekend and half the school vacations.

Winning is all that matters. My mother got everything in the divorce: the house in Colombes, the furniture, the dishes—even her in-laws' silver—the family photo albums, and, of course, the children. My father ended up with a tiny two-bedroom apartment in Nanterre.

The bunk beds in our room creaked endlessly. It was all he could afford on his mechanic's salary once he'd paid alimony and child support.

Winning is all that matters. I've always adored my father, even though his apartment was way too small for the games of hide-and-seek we were used to. Even though, when I was thirteen, I couldn't bear to tell him I was too old for his games. Even though I was sometimes embarrassed of him as a teenager, so embarrassed of his modest means that I wouldn't bring friends over on his weekends; I preferred to invite them to the house in Colombes, to the reassuring environment my mother provided for my sister and me, showering us with gifts and new clothes without worrying about her bank account. The alimony made it possible, and she would have done anything to feel like we preferred her to *him*, the homebody who had let himself slip into a routine that she suddenly, one day, couldn't stand anymore. My mother is an expert in one-upmanship. She always has to be the most generous, the most devoted, and the most well-liked parent.

Over the years, as puberty and its host of changes set in, I gave in to her cajoling and let myself be influenced. I got used to having everything I wanted when I wanted it, despite the fact that I had never been fooled by my mother's strategy. I took advantage of the situation without a hint of guilt; I figured she owed me at least as much for throwing my father out of the house and sentencing me to spend my life traveling between two homes, neither of which really felt like one anymore. I took everything my mother would give, but my disdain and indifference only grew. And when I didn't get what I wanted, I was ready with an underhanded comment about how I was thinking about going to live with my father—even when I had absolutely no intention of doing so. I knew exactly what buttons to push; I'd been expertly schooled in emotional blackmail.

Winning is all that matters. Without ever letting it show, I always stayed loyal to my father. I stayed loyal to him while taking advantage of the divorce and of the woman I held responsible for ruining our family. Ungrateful, maybe, but loyal.

My mother is the one who gave me this hunger for victory. I play to win: anything less is not for me.

But now I don't know what to do or think anymore. Why can't that girl just hop onto a plane and go? She's been saying that's her dream since the beginning, hasn't she? And Gabriel's not even really trying to keep her. She's clingier than a mussel stuck to a boulder. This thing keeps dragging on and on. It's like something out of a bad nineties soap opera.

So now what? I've lost? Am I just supposed to admit defeat and be a good loser? Do I really have to accept that I bet on the wrong horse, and now I've lost everything?

GABRIEL

It's four thirty in the afternoon and the light is already starting to dwindle. It will be completely dark before long. Gabriel is sitting on Chloé's grave, his back against the tombstone bearing his wife's name. The cemetery employee has walked past him several times with a severe look on his face to convey that a grave is not a bench and that it's outrageous to behave as if it were. Gabriel ignores him and watches as the last of his cigarette burns up in the fading light. He's meeting Emma at a restaurant at seven o'clock. He left work at four today, but given the amount of overtime he's put in over the years, no one could hold it against him.

"So, Chloé, what do you think about all this? Are you rolling over in your grave?"

He laughs at his own bad joke, then gets serious again.

"Who were you really anyway? Did you have me fooled all those years? Did you make a mockery of me with Simon? Why did you marry me and move to Saint-Malo if I wasn't enough for you? Why did you abort our baby without talking to me first? Was it mine at least? Did you hesitate before doing it, or did the idea of keeping it never even cross your mind?"

Gabriel throws his cigarette butt into the distance. It lands in a potted plant on another grave. Who cares?

"You're dead, and you left me behind. You got off scot-free, and I'm stuck here with all my questions and your dirty secrets. I'm suffocating from the weight of the doubt, and you're gone. What else will I find out in the coming months, huh? How many lies, how many betrayals will I discover?"

Gabriel loosens his tie.

"What do you think of Emma? I'm sure you wouldn't like her. She's not 'girly' enough for you. You always wanted luxury everything, and Emma is about the simple things in life. I'll admit that I knew that about you going in. You were always talking about money and jewelry and vacations. For you, to live was to spend. I thought you'd get tired of it, that I could fill that void in you. But now I understand that you can't make someone happy by taking away their dream, no matter how trivial it is. You can't change people. Believe me, I would rather have figured this all out before you died. I won't make the same mistake twice. Even if that means I have to suffer."

He lets out a snide laugh.

"You have no idea what I'm talking about, do you, Chloé?"

When he gets to the restaurant, Emma is already seated with a glass of white wine. She's rapping her fingers on the tablecloth, a pensive look on her face.

"Have you been waiting long?"

"About fifteen minutes. I finished my photo session early. The baby wouldn't stop screaming and the parents finally gave up. I'm not sure I'll be able to get anything decent from the shots I took."

Gabriel calls the waiter over and orders two flutes of rosé champagne. The man hurries back to the bar to fill the order. Surprised, Emma looks at Gabriel.

"Champagne? What are we toasting?"

"You," he offers mysteriously. When the waiter comes back with the glasses, Gabriel asks for menus. "I'm starving. How about you?"

Emma nods. She glances at the menu and chooses the sea bass à la plancha. Gabriel opts for a roasted rack of lamb with a thyme rub.

"This is no hole in the wall!" exclaims Emma, trying to lighten the atmosphere. The air around them is heavy, but she can't put her finger on why.

He takes her hand gently in his, then turns it over and lightly runs his thumb over her eagle tattoo.

"*L'aigle noir, dans un bruissement d'ailes, prit son vol pour regagner le ciel,*" Gabriel sings quietly. "With a rustle of its wings, the black eagle took flight to rejoin the sky."

"What did you say?"

"You chose to get a black eagle tattooed on your arm for the Barbara song, right?"

Emma is taken aback. She pauses before asking, "What song?"

Gabriel doesn't answer. He shakes his head to let her know it's not important. With Emma's hand still in his, he clears his throat.

"I have something for you."

"A present?"

"Yes, a present."

"But Christmas was a week and a half ago! And you've already spoiled me enough . . ."

Gabriel had gotten her silver earrings in the shape of two tiny cameras that she'd quickly put on.

"No, the earrings were only a taste of things to come."

Gabriel lets go of Emma's hand to take something out of his inside jacket pocket.

EMMA

A ring!

He's about to pull out a ring! I knew it!

He's been so mysterious for the past week. I could tell he was plotting something. I've been hoping I was right and trying not to think about it too much at the same time. I was so afraid of being disappointed, of getting my hopes up for nothing . . .

I admit that yesterday afternoon I ransacked the house while Gabriel was at work, looking for a little dark-blue velvet box with an engagement ring inside. I should know better, but even as a kid I would search the house top to bottom a few days before Christmas to find out what presents I was going to get. Old habits die hard!

I looked in the coffee-table drawer and scoured the living-room bookcase. Nothing. I ran to open his nightstand drawer and went through all his pants pockets. Empty. I checked the bathroom cabinet with Lucky on my heels—the poor dog must've thought I was hunting for dog treats.

Then, when Gabriel came home after work, I let him walk the dog by himself. I watched from the kitchen window as he left, and as soon as he turned the corner, I grabbed the car keys he hung in the entryway. I emptied the glove box, the driver-door storage space, and even took a quick look in the trunk—you never know. Nothing, nothing, and nothing.

I took advantage of the few minutes when he was in the bathroom, brushing his teeth and getting ready for bed, to go through the pockets of the jacket and pants he'd worn that day. Still disappointingly empty (unless I count the crumpled gum wrapper and used bus ticket I found).

In the end, I gave up and decided to wait for the big reveal. The fact that he had made reservations at a fancy restaurant for the following day was another good sign. I tried to get it out of him, but he wouldn't budge. Not even a hint. I feel a bit guilty, of course. But I'd rather not think about that for the time being.

And now the moment's here at last.

I want to jump up and down when he orders two glasses of champagne, but I manage to keep my cool.

What if he waits until dessert? I won't be able to eat a thing!

When he says he has a present for me, I want to squeal with joy, but I stay calm. I ready my face to express feigned surprise and genuine happiness. "Oh, Gabriel, I never would have expected it! How did you keep it a secret?"

He's hunting for something in his jacket, in the same pocket I went through last night. Maybe he's been keeping the ring at his office to make sure I wouldn't happen upon it.

"This is for you."

Gabriel places a pastel-green envelope on the table. He studies my face, which conveys genuine surprise and feigned happiness. I don't think there can be a ring in there. Unless it's an IOU?

"What is it?"

"Open it," he says invitingly as he pushes it toward me.

I gently slide my index finger under the flap. Inside I find a glossy envelope with immediately identifiable dimensions. And within that, a single plane ticket.

Paris–Tel Aviv. Open date.

One-way.

Tears fill my eyes against my will. I clench my teeth.

"Why?"

"Because you have to pursue your dream, Emma. Your place isn't here. You know that."

"But . . ."

"And I can't bring anything valuable to your life. I'm far from done grieving. Chloé is still too present in my thoughts for me to ask you to stay with me."

"So you're just making the decision for me?"

The shock that at first froze the blood in my veins has suddenly turned into anger.

"That's it for us, then?"

Gabriel sighs. "It's better this way, Emma."

Furious and humiliated, I get up to leave as the waiter brings us our food. Gabriel tries to keep me from going, but I ignore him.

I hurry back to his house, grab my suitcase from the back of the closet, and start messily throwing my things into it. I take all the important things and fill the trunk and backseat of my car as quickly as possible. I place the keys on the entryway table and give Lucky one last pat before closing the door behind me.

I sit down in the driver's seat, turn the key in the ignition, then pound both fists on the steering wheel.

I don't have anywhere to go.

CHAPTER 13
JANUARY 9, 2014

CHLOÉ

I've been debating whether to wear my hair down or up in a ponytail for hours. Gabriel has always liked my hair down, but then again, I wear it in a ponytail 75 percent of the time—it's just so *me*.

In the end, I pull it through a bright-pink hair tie.

I'm both excited and worried. As I climb out of the van and head up the gravel walkway to Gabriel's house—our house—my stomach is full of butterflies and my heart is racing. Blood rushes to my temples. Boom, boom, boom. I take a deep, determined breath, smooth a rebellious strand of hair behind my ear, and ring the doorbell.

I get a bark in reply. I'd forgotten about that damn dog.

The wait seems endless. I still don't know what I'm going to say or how I'm going to act.

Finally, after a few minutes that seem to last hours, a disheveled Gabriel opens the door partway. When he sees me, he freezes. I can almost hear the cogs in his brain grinding away, trying desperately to find some sort of rational explanation for what he must think is a hallucination.

My husband stands stock still.

"It's me, Gabriel, I'm back . . ." I offer softly, as if speaking to a man I'm trying to talk down from a rooftop. I edge closer. Slowly, to avoid scaring him.

"Chloé?" he mumbles in a hesitant voice. His eyes are open wide. He must be afraid that if he closes them I'll disappear.

"Yes, I'm here. Everything's going to be fine now. It's over."

I gently place my palm on his cheek. He shivers and takes my hand in his to make sure it's real. He wants to speak, but the shock is clearly preventing him from forming coherent questions.

"Can I come in?"

My husband takes a step back to let me through the doorway.

Home at last.

I notice the dog make a break for the kitchen. Apparently animals can sense emotions other than fear: from a single glance, he could tell that we'd never be friends.

Gabriel hasn't moved an inch. A statue.

"Are you coming?"

He jumps at the sound of my voice and closes the front door.

As he turns toward me, he seems to have snapped out of his stupor.

"You're . . . alive?"

I laugh. "Of course I'm alive. Did you think my ghost had come to your doorstep?"

He studies me, unable to understand what's happening.

"Come sit down in the living room, sweetheart."

Robotically, he follows me. I sit on the couch. Even though I'm in my own home, I have the peculiar impression that I'm *making* myself at home.

I lick my lips as I think about the best possible way to explain what's happened. I've gone over this moment dozens of times in my head, but now that it's here I don't know how best to handle Gabriel, who's staring at me, completely bewildered.

I decide to just go for it. Better to get it over with.

"It was all a game; a reality TV show. They faked my death and orchestrated your meeting another contestant, who had six months to get you to propose to her. Ridiculous, right? When the producers contacted me to explain the rules, I knew right away that we'd win. That you'd be incapable of moving on so quickly."

Gabriel opens his mouth but nothing comes out.

"And if she lost, we'd win five hundred thousand euros. Can you believe it? Half a million euros for six months of our lives! It's crazy, isn't it?"

I can't help feeling exhilarated, despite the fact that my husband seems totally indifferent. "Do you understand what I'm saying, Gabriel? We won. We'll be able to make all our dreams come true!"

I don't know how to get him to react. Especially since I was sure he'd hug me close and spin me around, shouting with glee. Looks like I was wrong.

"Honey? We're rich. We're *rich*!"

And then, the last thing I would ever have expected: Gabriel starts to cry. Not tears of joy, no . . . He's sobbing like a baby.

Then his tears give way to near-hysterical spasms.

I watch my husband and try hard not to roll my eyes. This is beyond me.

Just then, the cameras burst in.

GABRIEL

"Hello, Gabriel. We know that right now you must feel like your whole world has come crashing down. Could you share your initial reaction while it's still fresh in your mind?"

He looks up to see two cameramen alongside a blonde bimbo holding out a microphone, a wide smile plastered on her face.

He slowly wipes the tears from his cheeks.

"What emotion are you feeling most intensely now that you have your wife back? And last but not least, what's it like to suddenly discover you've managed to win five hundred thousand euros without even lifting a finger?"

The blonde is getting impatient. She sends several exasperated looks Chloé's way, but Chloé just raises her eyebrows defeatedly.

The microphone is still bobbing around just under Gabriel's chin.

He stands up suddenly, forcing the woman to step back. At five feet five inches tall, she realizes that Gabriel is at least two heads taller.

"You can either show yourselves out of my house immediately, or I'll show you out myself—the hard way. You have five seconds to make your choice," Gabriel threatens.

"No, wait. Don't take it personally . . . Don't you have a sense of humor? I was only ask—" objects the blonde.

"Five . . . four . . . three . . . two . . . one."

Gabriel moves toward the production assistant and grabs her arm. One of the cameramen comes over to defend her, while the second keeps filming.

Chloé tries to intervene.

"Gabriel, it's stupid to react like this. Really, think about what you're doing, please . . ."

Gabriel continues to head for the front door, dragging the blonde behind him, then suddenly seems to change his mind and lets go of the woman's arm. She glares at him for a millisecond, then regains her composure and plasters a toothpaste-commercial smile back on her face.

He climbs the stairs to the second floor. "Come up when you've gotten rid of them," he tells Chloé, without bothering to turn around.

He goes into the bedroom and sits down on the bed he hasn't slept in for months, ever since he'd moved to the fold-out bed in the guest room with Emma.

A few minutes later, Chloé shows up in the doorway. Gabriel can tell she's feeling hesitant and a little bit angry. He shakes his head in disdain.

"Do you think this was worth it?"

"You don't?"

"Did I deserve to believe you were dead for months, just for five hundred thousand euros? You have no idea what I've gone through! How you've made me suffer. Where were you this whole time, huh? Living the good life in the Caribbean, enjoying cocktails on the beach? While I was wasting away, believing that you had drowned."

Gabriel is yelling, and he's clearly furious.

Chloé explains as best she can. "The producers put me up in an apartment near Paris. It wasn't easy for me either . . . I hardly ever got to go out because they were so afraid I'd run into someone I knew, even though I kept telling them the chances were less than slim. I watched the videos they took of you. Sometimes live, which made me feel like I was still with you somehow, watching your everyday activities. Sometimes after editing, so I could get an idea of how things were going for you."

"Are you telling me that there are cameras everywhere? This has got to be a joke!"

"No, they put cameras up in the house, on my authorization of course. That's it. At least I think it is. And the other candidate had a hidden camera on her at all times."

"Emma?"

"I'd forgotten her name, but yes, I suppose so."

Chloé stops talking. She seems to be waiting for Gabriel's questions. He's wandered over to the window and is staring out into the distance.

"But I saw you . . . I saw you *dead*. At the morgue, on the autopsy table," Gabriel pleads as he runs his hand over his mouth and turns toward Chloé with a disgusted look on his face.

"They had pros do my makeup. The same people who do the makeup for the fake cadavers on crime shows. The show paid the coroner to play along and let them use the morgue. He only lifted the sheet for a few seconds, and you turned away so quickly. I was concentrating on keeping my breathing to a bare minimum."

"Did . . . Did everyone but me know? Am I the punch line of this sick joke?"

"No, that's why they made me leave Saint-Malo! Nobody knew, nobody at all. My funeral was no masquerade. Well, you know what I mean . . ."

Chloé appears to be losing track of her arguments and feeling less confident under Gabriel's harsh gaze.

"And how the hell do you think it made me feel to see you flirting shamelessly with that woman just a few weeks after my death? To see her moving into our house so quickly, as if I'd never existed? Do you really think that didn't hurt? I have feelings too . . ."

"Don't try to twist things around, Chloé. You're not very good at playing the victim," says Gabriel, his voice like ice.

"I did it for us," Chloé offers resentfully.

"Really? And what about Simon? And the baby? Did you do that for us too?"

Chloé's jaw drops. She's speechless.

EMMA

I had no choice but to get a hotel room last night. This morning I called the owner of the studio I'd been staying in before to explain that in the end, if it wasn't too late, I'd like to rent the place for a while longer. He hadn't found a new tenant yet, so he immediately took me up on my offer. I moved all my stuff out of my car into a big pile in a corner of the studio. I don't have the strength to put anything away, since I don't know how much longer I'll be staying in the city.

It's one o'clock, and I haven't had anything to eat or drink since the glass of champagne last night. Regardless, I couldn't stomach a thing.

By now Gabriel must have learned the truth. His wife must have shown up at dawn to tell him the good news. He could be in shock, or angry, or disappointed.

But he'll get over it. For half a million euros, you can get over anything.

He'll forgive his wife and forget about me quickly, convinced that it was all fake, that I was motivated by greed alone.

"Where Is My Mind?" starts playing, and I hold my breath as I rummage through my purse in search of my phone.

"Mom" comes up on the screen.

She always calls at the worst possible moment. I let it ring until my voice mail picks up. All this for nothing.

He'll never believe that I'm really in love with him. Sure, in the beginning, it was a game, a stupid game that would have helped me make my dreams come true . . . But as the weeks and months went by, I fell for him.

I forgot about the cameras. I forgot that at midnight on January 8 my dress would turn to rags and my carriage would turn back into a pumpkin if my prince hadn't asked me to marry him.

Or maybe I didn't really forget, I just chose to go along with it and enjoy the ride, because I had no choice in the matter anymore. The studio had made me sign a six-page confidentiality agreement, detailing all the things I wasn't allowed to reveal about the game—under threat of legal action.

I was trapped. I know, it's easy to say that now. Gabriel would laugh in my face if I sang him my sad little song. I don't know how to prove that what we had together was *real*. Especially since he backed away on his own last night when he handed me that plane ticket.

I'll give it a few days. I need time to think carefully about what I'm going to say, and he needs time to come to terms with everything he found out this morning. Is there any chance he'll forgive me? I kept blinders on for months, refusing to think about the inescapable end to this whole story, convincing myself that his feelings for me would be enough to conquer all the lies. *My* lies. "You should have thought of that before . . ." I shake my head to quiet my mother's chastising voice. I know I should have thought more about the consequences before signing up for the show, that I should have thought about how it would feel for Gabriel instead of just thinking of it as a kind of lottery.

Still, I can't help but feel like it should be a thousand times easier to forgive me than to forgive Chloé.

I hope that he'll be able to look beyond the surface, that he'll have enough perspective to remember what we had with each other. I hope he'll realize that I gave up the job I was offered to stay with him. That I postponed, yet again, the one thing I've always wanted so we could have a chance. He has to take a sacrifice like that into consideration, right?

What we had was real. I want so badly to believe that he won't let himself be influenced by the money, that he won't choose the easy way out . . .

I absentmindedly take off the charm necklace containing the hidden camera that's been filming nonstop for the past six months. I don't need it anymore.

CHAPTER 14
INTERMISSION

LUCILLE

My name is Lucille Bellanger. I've been an assistant director at Interference for just over two years. This is the first time I've ever been in charge of a reality show and I'm thrilled, especially since a leading channel has bought the rights for primetime broadcast!

I must say that the game we've come up with is truly innovative; it's not easy to develop original ideas given the number of reality shows already out there. The concept behind *Till Death Do Us Part* is extremely simple. The first contestant—the wife—makes her husband believe she's dead. The second contestant—the challenger—then tries to seduce the young widower. She has exactly six months from their first meeting to get him to ask her to marry him. If she succeeds, she wins five hundred thousand euros; if she fails, the wife gets the prize money.

We obviously didn't choose our contestants out of a hat. Given the number of applications we received, we had any number of choices. I knew right away that Chloé and Gabriel would be perfect. They met all the basic criteria, of course. They'd been married for over five years, which meant we could be relatively sure they were a strong couple. And they were young and attractive—you have to give viewers a reason to keep watching, something to fantasize about.

In addition to all that, Chloé was the ideal contestant: sure of herself and her husband, arrogant and vain enough to agree to the charade we had planned. She wanted the money so badly (how naïve do you have to be to think half a million euros will change your whole life?) that we knew nothing could make her change her mind—not even seeing her husband destroyed by her death.

Gabriel was the faithful and devoted husband, ready to sacrifice everything for his wife. The kind of romantic man who becomes the shadow of his other half. Exactly what we were looking for. We definitely didn't want a ladies' man who'd go out and sleep with another woman the night of his wife's funeral. We wanted some degree of resistance and emotional strife to keep things suspenseful, to keep viewers glued to their screens for the next episode.

As for Emma . . . Physically, she was exactly what we were looking for: very attractive in her own right, but Chloé's polar opposite. Naturally pretty instead of elegantly made-up. A kind of gamine rebel who reminded us of Jean Seberg. With that impish, spontaneous air about her that so many men adore—don't ask me why. But her naïveté was what first attracted our attention. She was totally sincere when she said she wanted to win the money to travel abroad as a photojournalist. We only half listened to her little speech about freedom, independence, and her passion for her art—that's not what interested us. It was the fact that she would do anything to make her dreams come true and that she seemed totally oblivious to the moral repercussions of the show. She never showed any sign of understanding that we were asking her to lead someone on, to use his weaknesses, to *manipulate* him. Her innocence was so extreme it was laughable. I never would've thought that anyone could be so incredibly naïve in this day and age. I don't think she ever even considered the consequences of what she was about to do. What really sealed the deal, though, was that behind all that talk about being committed to her art, she was clearly the kind of girl who would fall hard for the first nice, lonely guy she met. I like to call it the Mother Teresa phenomenon: the urge to save every unfortunate man who comes her way. The very first time I met Emma, I knew she'd grow to care about Gabriel, despite her best efforts not to. The show's psychologist had a session with her up front and did a personality test that confirmed all my suspicions. We didn't want a heartless temptress. The goal was for the viewers to watch as the love story blossomed between the two characters, for them to *believe in it*.

Don't act all shocked: everyone knows perfectly well that the plot is planned out before things get under way for this kind of show! There's no room for improvisation; we can't just let the cameras roll without knowing what will happen. There's a lot of money on the table. You have no idea how much it costs to produce a show like *Till Death Do Us Part*! With the hidden cameras, Chloé's upkeep for over seven months, and the salaries for the editors, extras, makeup artists, producers, and more, it all adds up to several million euros.

So it's true that we look for contestants with a particular psychological profile. Though *they* might not know how things will turn out, we're perfectly sure of the outcome.

We saw Chloé as a real wife-zilla. A bossy, superficial control freak. Viewers would start to wonder why her husband ever married her.

Gabriel was Mr. Nice Guy. The romantic yes-man who slowly learns to love again after his wife's sudden and devastating death.

And Emma, as I've already explained, was the happy, innocent girl next door.

The one who was supposed to win.

That was our plot. Gabriel would ask Emma to marry him and everyone gets a happy ending. Except for Chloé, of course, but no one would care since she deserved it for tricking her husband into thinking she was dead.

To ensure the expected outcome and keep the pace up when things started to get slow, we sometimes had to manipulate reality—only a little bit. Nothing too big. We cheat a smidge; it's nothing to write home about.

At the funeral, an extra encouraged Gabriel to attend the group therapy sessions where Emma would be volunteering. After all, they had to meet somewhere. We wanted a truly authentic feel to the show, so we decided to infiltrate a bereavement organization incognito, with *real* people and *real* suffering. It's way better than hiring actors.

We gave Emma index cards detailing all Gabriel's likes and dislikes. We had to give her a leg up if she was going to have any sort of chance of getting the "widower" to fall for her so quickly.

We made up the story about Simon when he showed up at the funeral. Chloé had told us who he was and about their shared past, which prompted us to make Gabriel believe his wife was still cheating on him. A gentle nudge to get him into Emma's arms that much faster.

As for the abortion, we hesitated for a long time before doing that. Not for any sort of ethical reason, but because we were afraid Gabriel would call the hospital to learn more. And by that point, we didn't have any money left to bribe doctors, especially since they generally come with big price tags—even the provincial hick variety.

But we decided to go for it anyway because we knew it would do Gabriel in. He'd always dreamed of starting a family, so he could never forgive his wife for depriving him of a child without at least mentioning it to him. Guess you could say we brought out the big guns! Chloé thought she was omniscient, that she was seeing everything as it happened, that we would *actually* show her everything . . . I have a hard time understanding how people can be so damn gullible. It gets tedious sometimes.

Okay, sure, I'll admit it: after that things got *a bit* out of control.

We led Emma to believe that a big NGO wanted to hire her, knowing full well that she couldn't accept due to the terms of the contract she'd signed with us. The idea was to put Gabriel in a situation where he needed to make her stay, to get him to realize that he could lose her, and to finally ask her to marry him. Honestly, I think we did everything possible to help the guy out.

Unfortunately, we hadn't planned on him suggesting that she go. I mean, really, how many men do you know who are willing to sacrifice their own happiness for the woman they love? It's the kind of thing you only see in romcoms, not in the real world! "Live your dream, honey. I don't want to be the one to hold you back." Blah, blah, blah. God, just thinking about it makes me want to puke.

That idiot screwed up the whole damn show.

Right now we're working on final edits for the show, which is scheduled for broadcast in early April. A little romance to celebrate the beginning of spring. We're trying to decide what to keep and what to cut, now that our plan has totally blown up in our faces. We're hoping to film a few positive clips of Chloé, to get the viewers to like her, to side with her more than Emma. But it's not going to be easy, especially since we can't use any "daily life" footage because she's out of the picture for six months. We're going to do short close-ups on aspects of her life before the game, interview the people who love her, maybe fabricate a volunteer position for her at the Humane Society or something like that. You know, cast her as likable. We'll film interviews with her to show how devastated she is as her husband gets closer to Emma.

I really think we can make it work and land on our feet. We just have to put things together right, add a narrator who makes Chloé look good, and that'll be that.

It's going to be the show of the season, just you wait.

This all stays between us, okay?

CHAPTER 15
FEBRUARY 2014

CHLOÉ

It's been a month since I "came back to life."

I've gotten back into swimming and running. I got my job at the gym back too, though I only plan on staying until we decide exactly what we'll do with the money. The girl they'd hired to replace me didn't make it past her trial period. Not peppy enough, or not hot enough. Elise looks at me with respect now. I don't know if it's because she admires the guts it took to fake my death for months or because she knows I might be rich—I can't tell everyone for sure until after the show has aired. Maybe she thinks she'll get something out of being nice to me—as if I could be *bought*.

My father hasn't spoken to me since I told him what I did. Oriane doesn't even pick up when I call. I can easily imagine her condescending critique: "When will you ever grow up, Chloé?" My mom is—obviously—the only one who gets it. She thinks my idea was "stellar." I tried to explain that nobody has said "stellar" for at least thirty years, but it's no use. She does her best to reassure me whenever I talk to her about how difficult things have become with Gabriel. She says I just need to give him some time to process the whole thing, that he'll come back to me in the end. "If it's not for love at first, the money will reel him in. Don't worry, sweetie."

That doesn't change the fact that I've slept alone every night since I've been back. Every morning I wake up in our bed and look to my left, hoping that during the night my husband returned to the place he occupied for so many years. But he's determined to keep sleeping in the crappy fold-out bed in the guest room.

I've tried explaining in every possible way that I never got back in touch with Simon after we moved to Saint-Malo, but I can tell he still doesn't believe me. Simon sent me one e-mail after the move to see how I was doing. I sent a short reply telling him that everything was amazing, that I loved Brittany, and that I went swimming several times a week. Period. Is it my fault he showed up at my funeral? Or that the studio planted that stupid fake note to make Gabriel worry? That they fooled me too?

"This is a *TV show*, Chloé! We have to keep things fun, spice it up!" answered Lucille Bellanger in a carefree tone when I called to demand an explanation.

And the whole abortion story is the cherry on top. Even though Lucille begrudgingly confirmed to Gabriel that it was another lie, I swear he still has his doubts.

"I don't know what to believe, Chloé. Are you really all that surprised, given everything that's happened? I don't even know who you are anymore. I don't trust you right now, and even though I want to, I don't know how to start trusting you again. I feel like I spent eight years living with a stranger."

Make way for the melodrama.

"What if you *had* gotten pregnant? What would you have done?"

Gabriel's tone is bitter and borders on threatening. His face is tense, his fists clenched in frustration. I instinctively back up a few inches.

"What kind of question is that? I told you I've never had an abortion!"

"Okay, but if you had found out you were expecting, what would you have done?"

"I have no idea, since it never actually happened! You can't hold a decision I might have made against me!"

"So, potentially, you could've chosen to have an abortion without even talking to me."

"I never said that! You're twisting everything I say, Gabriel. Facts are all that counts. I never got pregnant and I never had an abortion, okay?"

"Whatever you say . . ."

He exudes disdain. His tone, his eyes, his slightly curled lips and defensive posture. His whole being is so full of . . . I struggle to find the word, but when I finally put my finger on it, it hits me like a bag of rocks.

He is full of *disgust*.

My own husband is disgusted with me.

We're going nowhere. I've tried to convince myself that with time, everything will be like before, but I'm starting to lose my patience. I've tried being kind and gentle. Crying and asking for forgiveness. Anger. I've tried to win him over with gifts. I even bought a bowl for his beloved mutt. Nothing is working. The distance between us just keeps growing. He hardly even looks at me. He's elusive and impossible to read.

He can't reject me forever, can he?

The team at Interference has made it even worse by having me meet with their psychologist. "You'll see, Chloé, reality TV is his specialty. He knows what you're going through and will understand," explains Lucille in a slimy, slithering tone that reminds me of a snake hypnotizing its prey.

From the minute we meet, I can tell that the small balding man and I aren't going to get along. His arrogant smile and the way he explains that he knows exactly what I've been through and have yet to overcome are revolting. As if I were just another contestant like the dozens or maybe hundreds of others he's seen over the course of his career. As if I weren't unique at all, just another *product*. A broken machine to be patched up in a hurry. I want to tell him that in just eight months I made more money than he makes in eight years. But I hold back, feigning humility and modesty.

He pulls a thick file of stapled documents out of a black leather folder and puts on a pair of round glasses.

"Have you had trouble sleeping since the show ended?"

"No, not really."

"Do you feel stressed or anxious? Often, sometimes, never?"

"Never."

"Do you feel sad or depressed? Often, sometimes, never?"

"Never."

Sitting with my knees crossed, I start restlessly kicking my top leg to signal my impatience. The balding psychologist doesn't seem to notice, or at least offers no reaction.

"Are we almost done here?"

"My only goal, Ms.—"

"It's Mrs.," I say, cutting him off. Apparently the idiot doesn't even know I'm married. He clearly spent a lot of time studying my file before I walked in. An impressive display of incompetence.

The pudgy little man takes off his glasses and cleans the lenses with a cloth. He's really taking his time—I can't help but think he's doing it on purpose. When he holds them up to the light to check his work, it takes all my strength not to stand up and leave the tiny room. But Lucille highlighted in bright yellow the clause of my contract requiring me to submit to a psychological assessment at the end of the show. She offered a predatory smile as she ran her index finger over the lines, explaining, "It's for your own good, you know . . . Gabriel and Emma led a relatively normal life during the game, but not you. You're important to us, Chloé. The well-being of our big winner is a priority for us!"

The psychologist puts his glasses back on and stares at me with faded blue eyes. The seconds tick by. If he's trying to impress me, he's failed. I'm just getting more and more annoyed.

"My only goal, Mrs. Hamon, is to make sure that you can go back to your normal life. I know that returning to reality can be complicated after what you've been through, after being isolated for several months and following your dramatic reunion with your spouse."

"I'm perfectly fine."

He nods, muttering a circumspect "mmm hmm," as he jots down a few notes. I try to read them, but his writing is terrible—totally illegible upside down.

I listen to him distractedly for another twenty minutes, lackadaisically answering his questions, each of which is stupider than the last. Finally, he closes his folder and sighs—apparently his job wears him out quickly—then pushes a scrawled-on piece of paper toward me.

"What is this?"

"A prescription. Nothing too exotic. Half a Paxil every morning. It's a very light antidepressant. And Xanax, if you're feeling anxious. It will help with the . . . transition."

"But I said I'm doing great, didn't I?"

"I heard you. I'm not deaf, just nearsighted . . . Take the prescription, okay? You never know."

His smile is laced with pity, and all I want to do is crumple his little piece of paper into a ball and stuff it down his throat. To shut him up, suffocate him.

Instead I put on an amiable, obedient face, tuck the prescription in my purse, and leave the room with dignity, thanking him as warmly as possible.

Hypocrisy is one of my strengths.

GABRIEL

"Today we're going to talk about an important part of the grieving process: anger. I hope you've taken the time over the past month to think about the things that make you angry. Would any of you like to share?"

Gabriel has continued to attend the group, since Edith agreed he could finish the full twelve-session cycle, even though it turns out that he didn't lose anyone after all. She understands that, in many ways, his wife coming back has put him in a difficult situation. Now that everything has changed yet again, he has to grieve his past from *before* the show. When he called and asked her in a flat voice if he could come to the next session as planned, she didn't have the heart to tell him he had no place being there.

She didn't have the slightest problem, however, leaving a cold message on the photographer's voice mail informing her that she was no longer welcome at Coping with Bereavement. Emma tried calling back a number of times, but Edith didn't answer. The young woman's excuses didn't interest her in the least.

The attendees glance furtively at one another. It's always hard to be the first to speak, to break the silence.

Gabriel decides to start. He has so much to say that he figures it's best not to wait for someone else to work up the courage to open his or her mouth.

"For the past month, I've been filled with anger. With rage, even. I'm mad at my wife for agreeing to participate in this stupid show without thinking for even a minute about the suffering it would put me through. For deciding that everything we'd built together could be swept away with the brush of a hand in exchange for a big check. I'm angry that she doesn't understand my reaction to her coming home. Apparently she thought I'd jump for joy at the idea that we were rich. How could I have been so wrong about her? Was I completely blind to her flaws all those years? Did I just ignore them? Maybe in some ways this is all *my* fault, maybe it's the price I have to pay for believing in her?"

Edith nods silently, encouraging Gabriel to continue. He shakes his head as if trying to free himself from his intrusive thoughts, then goes on, his jaw visibly tense.

"I'm also mad at Emma, of course. She toyed with me, my emotions, and my grief. She set a trap for me without ever seeming to have even the slightest regret. Then she simply disappeared from the face of the earth overnight, leaving me wondering if she ever really existed."

Gabriel takes a pack of cigarettes out of his pants pocket, then remembers he obviously can't smoke inside. He puts it down on the table and keeps talking, without making eye contact with anyone.

"I'm mad at all the people behind reality TV, who are prepared to do anything at all as long as it gets good ratings. I was manipulated, and now I feel totally powerless! I can't even stop the show from being broadcast because it turns out that I signed the authorization papers and contracts without knowing it. For Chloé's funeral, the mortician had me sign dozens of forms, so many that I didn't even read them. I was too upset and in too much of a hurry to get it over with. I guess it's my fault. I should have checked them."

"Anybody would have done the same in your position, Gabriel," Laura offers kindly. "How could you have possibly imagined for even a second that your wife wasn't *actually* dead?"

Marie-Hélène nods, horrified at the thought. They all seem to think that, in some ways, what Gabriel has been through is *worse* than really losing a loved one.

Edith waits for a lull, then explains, "I'm going to give each of you a piece of paper. I'd like you to indicate how angry you are with the different people in your lives. The scale goes from zero to ten, with ten being the angriest. I'll let you have a few minutes to complete your 'angerometers.' Then the idea is for us to come back to these at our last session in June, to see if your anger has begun to subside."

Gabriel contemplates the blank chart. At the bottom of the page, he writes "Chloé," then "Emma." Next he adds "the studio," a vague term covering everyone who participated directly or indirectly in *Till Death Do Us Part.*

From Chloé's name, he traces a line to the number seven.

From Emma's, the line runs to the number eight, because he feels like she betrayed him even more than his wife.

Six for the reality TV people.

Gabriel moves to hand his paper in, then changes his mind.

He adds "Gabriel" to the list of names and draws a line that goes beyond the number ten. Because he didn't see it coming, because he went along with everything like a sheep to slaughter, because he gave people his trust like children throw crumbs to birds. Because he doesn't know who he is anymore or what to believe.

Because he feels more bereft now than when he found out Chloé had "drowned."

EMMA

I gave Gabriel almost two months to mull everything over. I spent them doing nothing but thinking about him, but I didn't give in to my urge to call.

Yesterday, I decided that I'd waited long enough and gave myself permission to dial his number—which I still know by heart. After five seemingly endless rings, it went to voice mail.

Since then, I've tried calling four more times. In vain. In the end, I left a message asking him to call me back. "We need to talk about what happened." As soon as I said it, I realized that I couldn't possibly have come up with anything more clichéd.

Edith also refuses to take my calls. I haven't been able to tell her that my involvement with her association was sincere. But even if she had listened, I doubt she would have believed me.

Today, after getting Gabriel's voice mail yet again, I summoned the courage to do something. I have to see him. He needs to hear what I have to say. I can't give up without a fight, even though the odds are against me.

At a quarter to seven that evening, the time when Gabriel usually leaves work, I was waiting across the street from the Société Générale branch on Rue Clemenceau, leaning discreetly against the bus stop. I had a clear view of the entrance to the bank as I tried to ignore the drizzle that was leaving a fine layer of freezing cold raindrops on my face and clothes. I pulled up the collar of my leather jacket and shoved my hands deeper into my pockets without ever looking away from the glass doors.

As the minutes trudged by in slow motion, I realized I hadn't prepared anything, that I had no idea what I was going to do once Gabriel came into view on the other side of the street, no idea what I'd say. A rush of anxiety washed over me as I tried to find the right words, words that might actually get through to him.

A woman approaching quickly in a long dark coat with shiny metal buttons suddenly caught my eye. I moved aside to let her pass; she was using her umbrella like a shield against the gusting rain and must not have seen me. Strangely, though, as she neared me, the click of her high-heeled boots on the sidewalk slowed. When I looked up, the face in front of me was painfully familiar. I'd never seen her in person, but I immediately recognized Gabriel's wife. She held tight to her umbrella as I watched the rain drip over the sides in the light of the streetlamps. We sized each other up for what seemed like an eternity, like two boxers waiting for the perfect moment to throw the knockout punch.

"What are you doing here?" she finally asked curtly.

"I . . . I was in the neighborhood, and . . ." I exhaled calmly, telling myself not to be intimidated. I couldn't let her get the upper hand. "I need to talk to Gabriel."

I held my head up high and ran my fingers through my damp hair. I suddenly realized my Converse-clad feet were soaked. Chloé was clearly unshaken and sure of herself despite the uncomfortable-looking heels, which raised her several inches above the ground.

"I get it . . . He won't pick up when you call or answer your messages, is that it? So you've decided to make him listen to you, whether or not he actually *wants* or *needs* to see or hear from you. It's pretty sad to be reduced to something like this, don't you think?"

Chloé's gaze was full of pity, almost compassion. And all of a sudden I felt pathetic for spying on Gabriel outside his office.

"I just wanted to explain myself . . ." I said, hating my voice and suddenly submissive attitude.

Chloé's smile was almost kind.

"We played the game, Emma. But it's been over for a while now, and you know it. There's nothing worse than a sore loser. Those people who refuse to admit defeat, to accept that they weren't good enough, that they were bested by their adversary. It's downright embarrassing."

I feigned calm as my nails dug into my palms inside my jacket pockets. Chloé carefully replaced a few strands of her glossy hair before going on.

"But you know what? Instead of meeting up with my husband in a few minutes as planned, I'm going to turn around and go home. That way, you can try to talk to him, though I seriously doubt he'll even slow down when he sees you. I'm a good sport, so go ahead, try your luck. If you can manage to work up the courage, that is . . ."

Before I even had the chance to mumble anything in reply, Chloé had turned around and started walking back the way she'd come. Her stride exuded the confidence of a model on the catwalk. She must have known I was watching; she was used to turning heads.

A few minutes later, a man left the bank in the shadows. Gabriel. Without a glance at his surroundings, he turned left and headed up the street, into the wind.

My feet refused to move. There was no point.

As the weeks go by, I feel more and more like a pariah, hiding out in my tiny apartment, waiting for God knows what. I still haven't told my parents about the show. I'm too afraid of my mother's reaction. She would have understood, or at least accepted my choice to participate in the show if I'd won the five hundred thousand euros, but now I'm sure she'll see it as a waste of time at best. "Emma, how could you have toyed with someone else's feelings like that? Didn't your father and I teach you better?" I still have a bit of time before the show airs to find a better way to explain the whole thing. Or maybe by some miracle my parents will never hear about the show?

After my run-in with Chloé, I decided to accept the job in Gaza, but when I called the HR guy who contacted me back in December, a metallic voice told me the number had been disconnected. Could I have been any more naïve? Did I honestly think that the manipulation would stop with Gabriel?

All's fair in love and war, I suppose.

So what do I do now? Stay in Saint-Malo and keep hoping against hope that Gabriel will let me explain myself—that we'll get our happy ending? Go back to the boring life I had in Arles before coming here? Finally leave the country for anywhere but here to realize my dreams, without any money?

CHAPTER 16
MARCH 2014

CHLOÉ

Exactly a year ago, I was signing my contract at Interference.

I read through its dozens of clauses, my lips pursed in fake concentration, trying really hard to hide the fact that I didn't understand much of the legal jargon it was full of. Eager to get on with things, Lucille Bellanger asked casually if everything was clear. The only thing I took away from the stack of papers she'd given me was that thanks to Gabriel, I was going to be rich. I didn't realize that I was also agreeing to have cameras film our reunion and daily life for several months after the end of the contest. And it turns out that Gabriel also stupidly signed all the papers, when he thought he was instead choosing my casket and the location of my grave.

So we have no way out.

The circumstances make rekindling our relationship pretty difficult . . . I didn't plan on having to live my life on camera, in my own house, every second of every day.

I try to call Gabriel during the day so we can talk freely, but he rarely picks up. When he does, he gives me a curt, "I'm busy." In other words, "I don't want to talk to you," and "Leave me alone, I don't need you." I know, I read too much into the few words he actually says to me. To be honest, with every passing day I feel more lost about how to approach him. I wouldn't go so far as to say that I regret signing up for the show, but *almost*.

It's ridiculous, isn't it?

The five hundred thousand euros showed up in our checking account last week. Gabriel didn't mention it, but I know he must have noticed. I haven't dared bring it up again—when the studio's accountant called two weeks ago to tell me the transfer would be going through soon, Gabriel didn't react at all like I expected.

"You do realize you're completely delusional, right, Chloé?"

"What do you mean?"

"I feel like you must live on a different planet. Do you know what five hundred thousand euros buys today?"

I frowned, caught off guard.

"I don't understand what you're getting at. We can do all sorts of things with the money, the list is too long to go through!"

Gabriel, who was sitting on the couch, crossed his arms across his chest in a sign of contempt.

"Like what exactly? Go on vacation and buy some clothes and a new car? Really, please, tell me what you had in mind when you signed that contract."

His eyes went cold and the smirk on his face made me cautious.

"I don't like your tone, Gabriel."

"Oh, well, excuse *me*. I just think that maybe you didn't think it all through, that maybe some advice from someone who works in finance would have been useful at the time. But, hey, it's not like you're married to a 'banker' or anything, right?"

I somehow managed to keep an indifferent expression on my face and let him continue.

"I mean, do you really want to know what we can do with half a million euros? Let's say we buy a house here in Saint-Malo. We'd still have about two hundred thousand left. So, if we assume we can get by on two thousand a month, since the house would be paid for, it would last, oh, not even ten years. And that's if we don't change our daily life at all: we stay in Saint-Malo, don't spend unreasonably, don't take any trips, and don't make any big purchases. Nope, sorry to burst your bubble, but the truth is that five hundred thousand euros doesn't really change anything. We can't quit our jobs and leave everything behind. Champagne cocktails will not be a nightly occurrence. 'Half a million' might sound great, but nobody lives like a prince on so little."

I clenched my jaw, furious. I wanted to tell him to shove his numbers. There was no way I was going to let him win.

"Do you really think I didn't go through the figures myself? I'm afraid you're sadly mistaken. You know what, Gabriel? I think you're just bitter."

I turned around and left the room before he could continue his demonstration. And, more importantly, before he could see how shaken I was.

So this morning, weary of our stalemate, I've finally decided to ask him if he'd rather I leave.

"We don't have to live together if you can't stand me anymore. I don't know what else I can do to get my husband back. What's done is done, Gabriel. I want us to move forward together, but if we can't, then we should go our own ways . . . We can't keep on like this. There's no point. I can't snap my fingers and suddenly make you forgive me. I wish I could change everything with the wave of a magic wand, but that's not the way the world works. So if you can't stand to be around me anymore, just say so, once and for all."

He continues to wash the pile of dishes in the sink without looking up.

"I've put up with your anger, your sadness, and now your indifference. I've been tiptoeing around you, wondering how to get you to come back to me. What do you want me to do? What could I say to get you to listen, to forgive me? I made a mistake. Is that what you want to hear?"

Tired of talking to his back, I step closer and turn off the running water. He keeps scrubbing a pile of silverware, without even glancing at me.

"All right, get out a recorder, then: I made a mistake! I thought you'd be strong enough, that you'd also think participating in the show was worth it once it was all over, and I was wrong. Yet more proof that we never really know our loved ones as well as we think. I'm sorry."

No reaction, just the infuriating squeak of the sponge against the dish he's washing. My eyes start to fill with tears despite all my efforts.

"Please, I'm begging you, forgive me . . ."

The water in the sink is so hot that columns of steam fill the small kitchen.

"Did you hear me?"

I'm a ghost. How ironic.

I decide not to push him just then and head out for a run before going to work. I turn the volume on max and a rhythmic melody fills my eardrums. I time my stride to the heady bassline. I'm in the zone.

Could I even make sense of my life without Gabriel? When I decided to take the plunge with the show, I never thought for a second that the separation might be irreversible, that an irremediable rift would grow between us. But as the weeks fly by, I'm starting to doubt his ability to get over it all and forgive me. Maybe I overestimated him. He's so much more fragile than I am. So much more idealistic.

But every time I dreamed about what I would do with half a million euros, I imagined myself with Gabriel. I imagined the life we could build together if we were suddenly free of financial obligations. If money no longer factored into any of our decisions. Before Gabriel spelled it out for me, I didn't realize that five hundred thousand euros wouldn't really make us rich. That all we'd be able to do is buy a house—in some small town—and go on a few trips. I really thought we'd be able to quit our jobs and give our bosses the finger if we wanted.

Before I signed up for the show, I dreamed about everything we could do together.

Together.

I wonder if any of it was worth it if he's not by my side. What's the point of being rich without Gabriel?

I don't know how to tell him all this. I feel like he's forgotten who I am, like he doesn't know why he chose me to be his wife, why he loved me. I wish he would remember us rather than letting these few months erase everything we had together, but I'm powerless against his indifference. I want to stand up and scream, "It's me!" but I'm too afraid of his icy stare, which looks right through me without actually seeing me. "It's me . . ."

When I come home at the end of the day, exhausted after several cardio classes in a row, Gabriel has dinner waiting. Salmon lasagna. I recognize the enticing aroma wafting from the kitchen.

I drop my purse on the entryway floor and hesitantly make my way to the kitchen to join him. He comes over to me and looks directly at me, his face unreadable. I have no idea what he's feeling.

Then his lips finally move. "Truce?" he murmurs.

I nod suspiciously and sit down on one of the bar stools. *Truce? Really?* I feel like a fifth grader playing tag whose adversary has finally admitted defeat. Will this be a temporary break in hostilities, or a real end to the war? I guess only time will tell.

I keep my questions to myself and smile shyly. There's no way I'd risk ruining the moment with questions that could antagonize him. I prefer to take what he's willing to give. I almost feel like I'm on a first date. When you'd do anything to get the other person to like you and are so afraid of committing the slightest faux pas or letting conversation lag.

Gabriel pours me a glass of Sancerre and holds his glass to mine to toast.

"To us?"

GABRIEL

Gabriel had been tempted to rip out the cameras hidden in every room of the house, but Chloé convinced him not to if he wanted to keep the five hundred thousand euros. Though the money is of little interest to him, Gabriel is practical; he understands that it would be stupid to have gone through the entire masquerade for nothing.

Having spent his childhood with parents who started yelling and glaring at one another at breakfast every morning, he hates conflict. He always promised himself he'd never go through that again, no matter what. He's told Chloé everything he feels he needs to say, and isn't the kind of person to keep nagging her with the same critical comments over and over. And he can't stand the idea of their home becoming a theater of trench warfare. So he's decided to loosen up a bit and let Chloé slowly make her way back to him. He hopes that his overflowing emotions will abate with time, that soon he won't be so sensitive anymore. He hopes he'll be able to move forward.

He studies Chloé's bottles of nail polish lined up along the edge of the bathroom sink and runs his hand over her clothes, which are back in their closet. All around the house, he notices her things strewn about: her charcoal-gray sweater on the banister, a bar of white chocolate on the coffee table, her mug with a used tea bag on the kitchen counter. It's like nothing has changed, like nothing even *happened*.

As if everything were just like before.

He distractedly clears the table from dinner last night. While he waits, powerlessly, for the studio to finish filming, he feels like they've suspended his freedom. The only thing he's been able to do is refuse to be interviewed for *Till Death Do Us Part*. Chloé went along with their little charade, went on and on about how happy she was to have won, how excited and hopeful she was about being reunited with her husband and starting a new life together. For Gabriel there was just no way. He had been duped and refused to support any of it.

He's having lunch with Geoffrey today. Sandwiches and a walk in the park halfway between their respective offices. The weather is particularly nice for this time of year and the park is full of people out for a stroll.

"So, buddy, what's it like to be rich?" asks Geoffrey, eager to hear Gabriel's take on things.

"Doesn't change much."

"Doesn't change much? Hang on a sec! You must realize your life is going to change dramatically! Just think of everything you can do with that much money! If I had half a million euros, I'd leave everything behind. First of all, I'd stop slaving away five days a week for a pittance. Seriously, I'm sure that if you invested it you could live off the interest alone!"

Gabriel smiles. Geoffrey sometimes seems to forget that Gabriel's the financial advisor. He's already done all the calculations. He painted a particularly bleak picture for Chloé, to put her in her place. He talked about using most of it to buy a house outright, when in fact he knows all too well that it would be more advantageous to take out a loan. But trampling her exaggerated enthusiasm was just too tempting. When he had learned how far she was willing to go for money, he had felt so humiliated, so *pathetic*. And the day of that fight he wanted Chloé to feel the same way. To be shaken to the core, if only for a second, by a few simple calculations.

Geoffrey continues imagining what he'd do out loud, and Gabriel doesn't have the heart to set his friend straight. Objectively, even with a low-risk investment, he and Chloé could in fact earn a comfortable supplementary annual income—without lifting a finger. Not enough to live like sheiks, but enough to have some fun. It's a simple fact: money breeds money.

Geoffrey continues with his fantasy.

"I'd pack my bags and take a trip around the world for at least a year! Let me tell you, man, I'd take advantage of it! You and Chloé still don't have any plans?"

"We haven't had time to think about it yet."

"Don't tell me you're still mooning over that photographer woman! She used you, and now you need to move on!"

"How do you know? Maybe she was sincere."

"Have you spoken to her since January?"

Gabriel shakes his head. For the past several weeks, he's been routinely erasing the messages Emma leaves on his voice mail without even listening to them.

"And what difference would it make if she was sincere?" Geoffrey goes on.

"None. You're right. It wouldn't change anything at all."

If it was all just a game for Emma, there's no reason to pine for her. And if she really was in love with him, then the only choice is to let her go, like he did when he bought her the plane ticket. Emma isn't the kind of bird you can keep in a cage. Either way, Gabriel prefers not to talk about her.

"How are things with Chloé? Are you still sleeping in the guest room?" jokes Geoffrey.

"No. We're trying to pick up the pieces. It's going to take time, but we're both trying, so it should all turn out okay . . ."

"Aren't you being a bit melodramatic? I mean, sure, thinking she was dead couldn't have been much fun, but at a certain point you just have to forgive and forget, don't you think?"

"That's exactly what I'm trying to do."

Everything is always so simple for Geoffrey. He doesn't see why it's so hard to go back to the way things were after being manipulated for months. He doesn't understand that the thing that really bothers Gabriel isn't that Chloé lied to him, but that now he doesn't know how to trust her again. Seventy-five percent of the time he feels empty, as if a vampire sucked the life—his soul—out of him. As if he let the sharp fangs plunge into his neck without putting up a fight. He remembers something a childhood friend said to him once when Gabriel had turned down an invitation to a party in order to spend time with Chloé when they were still dating: "It seems like your life revolves around her . . . Sometimes it even feels like you *are* her!" The little voice in his head has been repeating the mild slight over and over for days.

He wonders who he is now. Who he would be if he had never met Chloé. If he would have become a different man without her.

Geoffrey's upbeat voice tears Gabriel away from his thoughts.

"Well, if you really don't know what to do with the money, you can always give it to me! I've got a thousand different ideas for spending it."

EMMA

Gabriel,
I've been sitting in front of this piece of paper for almost an hour, trying to decide what to say, but nothing seems right.
I'm writing this because you refuse to talk to me. Don't worry, it'll be my last attempt to contact you; I'm

not the kind of woman who harasses the man she loves. If you choose not to answer, I'll leave you in peace.

I doubt you'll believe any of what I'm about to write, but it's important for me to tell you the truth—my truth. The rest is up to you.

I agreed to participate in the show because I had always dreamed of becoming a celebrated photographer, and I wanted to have the means to leave everything else behind, to live my art without thinking about money. When I signed my contract with Interference, it was just like I was buying a lottery ticket. A chance to get rich quickly and easily. I didn't realize that I would be hurting someone in the process.

I know, I'm so naïve.

By the time I finally realized what I was doing, it was too late. I had signed the contract: I couldn't back out and I couldn't tell you the truth. So I kept going. I let myself get pulled in, and then I started to have feelings for you.

Over the weeks and months we spent together, I fell in love with you—despite myself. I wanted to tell you everything at least a hundred times. Even if you hate me now, you know I couldn't tell you. You know that in the end, we were all trapped.

I really do love you. And I'm truly sorry.

I don't know what else to say or how to prove my love for you, except maybe by reminding you that when I was given the opportunity to live my dream, I didn't take it. I chose you.

At a certain point during the show, I thought that if I won the five hundred thousand euros and still stayed with you, you would know that what we had was real, that it wasn't just a farce. I held on to that hope. But I lost . . .

Do you remember the framed picture of the two of us I gave you for Christmas? Open it, please. Inside you'll find a statement I wrote and signed back in December 2013, before the end of the show. In it I promise to share the money with you if I win. The document was drawn up by a lawyer and notarized, so there's no trap, no fraud. It's the only way I could think of to prove my sincerity to you if I lost.

I hope you'll be able to find the strength to forgive me.

I love you.

Emma

CHAPTER 17
APRIL 2014

CHLOÉ

When a letter came for Gabriel in the mail last week, I knew who'd sent it right away. A handwritten ivory envelope addressed to my husband. It was clearly a woman's writing. No return address, obviously.

My first impulse was to throw it out before Gabriel saw it. That little tease was part of the past now anyway. Gabriel and I were just starting to get closer, and I didn't need her back in the picture adding fuel to the fire.

But my curiosity got the better of me. I'd read enough detective novels as a kid to know how to discreetly steam open an envelope. I put a pot of water on the stove and watched as the seal slowly moistened and the flap came loose.

I skimmed Emma's flowery letter. It was like something out of a Harlequin novel. I really don't understand what Gabriel saw in her. I searched everywhere for the framed photo she mentioned, but gave up quickly. In the end, I decided it wasn't that important to find.

I gently refolded the letter, slid it back inside the envelope, resealed it, and placed it under two thick dictionaries to flatten it out so Gabriel wouldn't suspect a thing. Satisfied, I put it back with the other envelopes the mailman had delivered that day.

I didn't throw out the letter because I don't want to look bad if Gabriel ever finds out about it. And to be honest, when I really think about it, I don't consider Emma a threat. Sure, she managed to seduce my husband—actually, "seduce" is maybe a bit much—when he thought I was dead, but now I'm back. She doesn't stand a chance with me around. A six-month fling hardly compares to eight years together. It'll take Gabriel a little longer to really start trusting me again, but I know he'll get there. I know he doesn't want to throw away what we've built together over the years.

Lucille Bellanger's minions finally came by our house early last week to remove the hidden cameras. It took them a whole morning. I feel like a weight has been lifted now that I know my every move isn't being filmed anymore. Being on camera 24/7 is no way to live. I didn't sign up to be the new Truman Burbank . . .

I can tell Gabriel's breathing easier as well. He's been more spontaneous since the cameras came down. He's getting closer to me, really trying. We still have one last hurdle to jump before we can get back to normal life, though. The show is set to air in a few days: every Monday night at 8:50 p.m. for eight weeks. Personally, I'm excited to see myself on TV, but I know Gabriel is dreading it. It was hard enough for him to put up with his friends' and family's reactions and remarks about my reappearance, so I'm afraid it will be even worse when his acquaintances and colleagues see him on the show.

It'll be hard—for him. But afterward I'm sure we'll go right back to being perfectly unknown, as soon as another show takes our place. People will forget about us quickly, thanks to all the other things consumer society will keep shoving down their throats.

Maybe every once in a while someone—the baker, the appliance salesman, a client at the gym or bank—will say, "It's funny, but I'm sure I've seen you somewhere before . . ."

And the rest will be history.

GABRIEL

Gabriel hated all the sympathetic glances he got from his family and friends when Chloé died, but he really can't stand the ones he's been getting since *Till Death Do Us Part* aired on TV two weeks ago.

In the primetime slot. Obviously. That way the entire country gets a chance to feel sorry for him.

That morning at the grocery store, he even saw his face at the checkout stand on the cover of a *TV guide*. *Will Gabriel remain faithful to his wife or fall for the beautiful Emma?* It was a photo taken of him at the cemetery without his knowledge, during one of his visits to Chloé's fake grave.

Six more weeks and it'll all be over.

Chloé suggested they go away on vacation while the show is being aired, but Gabriel argued he couldn't leave the bank for two months, so they might as well face the sudden but temporary media frenzy head on.

Gabriel had cut his curly hair earlier this month, leaving less than a quarter inch behind. His wife doesn't care much for the new look, but he didn't ask her opinion. He pulls an old Nike baseball cap on when he leaves the house and avoids making eye contact with strangers in the street.

It's a different story with his clients at the bank. He often has to listen—or at least pretend to listen—to their advice, questions, and criticisms regarding the show.

"So who did you choose in the end? You can tell me, I promise not to tell anyone until the show's over!"

"Seriously, if I were you, I would've gone crazy when I found out I'd been used for months!"

"What about Lucille Bellanger? Is she nice? You've seen her up close, do you think she's had a nose job? I'm pretty sure she has . . ."

"Who won? I guess it wasn't you, since if you'd won, why would you still be working here? The photographer must have won the prize money and taken off to live her dream abroad . . ."

"If I were you I'd sue. It can't be legal to make someone be part of a reality TV show without his knowledge! If you want, I can recommend a friend of mine who's a lawyer. He's a shark. Hang on a second, I bet I have his number in my phone . . ."

"I just don't understand why people watch shows like that. Everyone knows it's rigged, so what's the point? Who knows, maybe you were even in on it! Come on, admit it!"

Gabriel does his best to end the conversations politely. His schedule is booked two months out—everyone wants him as their financial advisor. Andy Warhol's fifteen minutes of fame are dragging on a bit too long for Gabriel's taste.

Sometimes he wonders how Emma's handling her time in the spotlight. She seems to have disappeared from the face of the earth since he got her letter last month. He read it several times, but couldn't look in the frame to see if she was telling the truth even if he wanted to. He'd thrown the gift away along with everything else when he found out the truth about her in January. He got rid of everything she had left at his place, including her coffee maker, which she must have forgotten in her rush to move out after their last dinner together. It hardly mattered if she was telling the truth or not anyway. He didn't want to believe her anymore.

As for Chloé, she agrees to interviews with every journalist who calls, but she knows enough not to talk to him about them. When she comes home at night she never says a word about the show. He can tell she's doing her best to make it easier for him. He would like to be able to do the same for her, but doesn't know exactly how to go about it.

All he knows for sure is that the only thing to do now is wait.

And be patient.

EMMA

Wedding season is starting up again, but since the beginning of the month I've had nothing but cancelations. I should have predicted that: no one wants a heartless husband-stealer taking pictures at their wedding . . .

I have no work, and my meager savings are dwindling by the day. I won't be able to keep this up for long. Plus, it doesn't really make any sense for me to stay in Brittany. Gabriel's not coming back. I've hoped and waited long enough. I have to be realistic.

Lucille Bellanger called yesterday. She had an "un-be-*liev*-able" offer for me.

"I had a brilliant idea last night that I'm sure you're going to love! What would you say to telling Gabriel you're four months pregnant? You know, to keep things interesting! I did the math: that'd mean you got pregnant around December 25. You did make love over Christmas, didn't you?"

I refused to dignify the question with a response.

"We'll make you an adorable little silicone baby bump and a fake ultrasound to really get Gabriel going! At this stage of a pregnancy it already looks like a tiny baby with little arms and legs. It's *too* cute! I think you can even find out the sex at four months! Do you know if Gabriel would rather have a boy or a girl?"

The words just kept pouring out of Lucille Bellanger's mouth, like a never-ending avalanche. Her tacky enthusiasm had her so wound up that I struggled to get a word in edgewise.

"You have *got* to be out of your mind!"

"Not at all! Listen, I've thought it all through: you tell him you're pregnant, he comes back to you straightaway, and then a few weeks later you have a miscarriage. Ta-da, everything's peachy! All you'd have to do is console him yet again, and we both know you're good at *that*. He'd never suspect a thing!"

"But why in the world would you want to fake something like that? The game is over, they've already won the five hundred thousand euros. What more do you want?"

"Let's just say that . . . Well, I shouldn't really be talking to you about it, Emma, but the truth is that the show's not doing as well as we'd hoped. The first episode got promising ratings, but the next two fell flat. If we don't get back on track with some enticing trailers, viewers will lose interest and the show will get bumped to late night. It would be just *awful* to be forgotten after all our hard work . . ."

"And I should care about all this *why?*"

On the other end of the line, Lucille Bellanger stifled a laugh, seemingly surprised by my indignance.

"Oh, come on, Emma, I wasn't born yesterday, you know! I'd have to be blind not to realize that you really do care about Gabriel, that you practically fell in love with him the first time you met!"

"That's not true," I managed, but my voice was not very confident. I hated that I couldn't find the words to give this maniac a piece of my mind.

"There's no fooling me, I know what I saw. I could even tell you I planned it all! That's why we picked you in the first place, so be honest with me! I'm doing this to help you too, don't you see? It's a win-win. I would hate for your love story to end like this, and all because of a stupid misunderstanding. I want you to get your happy ending! You deserve it, especially after all you gave up . . ."

She softened her voice to a syrupy-sweet tone and I rolled my eyes. She really thought I was an idiot.

"I think we've said all we have to say, Lucille. I have to go."

Over the line, I could almost hear how fast she shed her best-friend mask.

"No, wait! Since you've forced my hand, let me put my cards on the table: I'll give you twenty thousand euros to play along with this harmless little game. You have to admit that's good money. I wouldn't offer this much to just anyone, believe me."

"I can't believe you'd think for a second that I'd accept!"

"I know that your financial situation is complicated. I just wanted to give you a helping hand, that's all! Don't tell me money doesn't interest you because I wouldn't believe you . . . So, you'll do it? I can have the funds transferred ASAP. I know that you can't afford to pass something like this up . . ."

I hung up without answering and turned off my phone.

That woman will stop at nothing.

If she keeps on like this, next thing I know she'll suggest I kill myself to make Gabriel feel guilty and give the viewers a chance to shed a few tears.

CHAPTER 18
MAY 2014

CHLOÉ

"You must be pretty disappointed that they canceled the show so suddenly, huh?" asks Oriane, clearly mocking me. It's the same arrogant tone she always takes with me, as if I were a stupid little girl.

She finally decided to call me back a week ago to say that if my husband could forgive me, then she should be able to do the same. That's why Gabriel and I drove all the way to Rennes to have lunch at her house with my nieces and nephew. Her husband, Maxime, isn't here, but there's nothing unusual about that. He's obsessed with historical reenactments and often spends entire weekends participating in medieval tournaments. I've never really understood the fascination, but I suppose he probably liked playing dress-up as a kid, and his hobby lets him continue doing it with other adults who are just as nostalgic as he is.

Oriane and I are comfortably seated on a glider in her huge backyard. Gabriel is playing Frisbee with Adrien and Alice, her two older children. My sister and I are talking as she feeds Léontine her strained vegetables. My niece keeps wriggling in her seat, clearly more interested in playing with her brother and sister than in swallowing the parsnip purée her mother has made.

"I don't care that *Till Death Do Us Part* was a flop. I didn't do it to become a TV star. I did it for the money. Plus, Gabriel is so relieved that the whole thing ended after only a few weeks on the air."

After the third episode, the show was bumped from 8:50 p.m. to 11:10 p.m. Then, given its poor ratings, the network canceled it altogether—much to Lucille Bellanger's chagrin. After all, her career was on the line.

"Come on, Léontine, one more bite and you can go play Frisbee too."

Oriane flies the small silver spoon around like an airplane. The toddler follows it with her eyes, a sour look on her face. When the food nears her mouth she reluctantly opens and chews up the vegetables as she watches her brother throw Gabriel the Frisbee.

"How are things between you two?"

Oriane has put on her concerned-big-sister face. I hate it when she does that, but at least I know she's sincere.

"Things are much better. I think the show and my 'death' are finally behind us. I'm sure that in a few months it'll all be just a fading memory for Gabriel."

"You do regret signing up for such a twisted contest, though, don't you?"

I watch as Oriane wipes Léontine's mouth. I'm disappointed by her question, but not surprised. My sister will never get me.

"Not in the least! Gabriel and I are rich. We don't have to worry about money ever again! We can do whatever we want without a second thought."

Oriane keeps quiet. I bite my lower lip self-consciously. There's no way I'm admitting to her that I'm hardly made of money. I don't know if she's silent because she doesn't want to rain on my parade, or because, like me a few weeks ago, she doesn't realize that it's not enough for Gabriel and me to laze around the Bahamas for years.

"If I'd lost Gabriel, maybe then I'd regret becoming a contestant, but look: in the end, everything's turned out fine between us. Why would I have regrets?"

"If you say so. Well then, what are you planning to do with the money?"

"We have tons of ideas! First, we're going away for a whole month this summer. We haven't decided exactly where yet, but definitely somewhere with sunny beaches. Maybe Costa Rica; we hear it's amazing. A vacation will do us both a lot of good. I've already bought a couple of new bathing suits for the occasion."

Léontine clambers down from her high chair and runs over to the others, squealing with joy.

"After that, who knows . . . I'd like to move back to Paris. I can't see myself living in Saint-Malo forever. In the winter the place feels deserted; it's depressing after a while. But I haven't talked to Gabriel about it yet. I'm not sure he'll be as excited as I am about heading back, so I'll wait awhile before suggesting it. I'll bring it up after our vacation. But one thing is sure: I can't keep wasting away in that small provincial town for much longer."

Alice comes over and sits down between her mother and me to pout.

"What's wrong, sweetheart?"

"Léontine doesn't know how to play Frisbee. She holds it instead of throwing it. I *hate* her . . ."

"Excuse me?" asks her mother with a scolding look on her face.

"I mean I don't *like* it when she does things like that," Alice corrects herself.

"You have to be patient, honey, she's still little. You have to let her have some fun too, okay?"

Alice crosses her arms over her chest and lets out a loud sigh.

I look over at Gabriel. He's throwing Léontine up into the air as she gleefully screams, "Again, again!" before she even falls back into her uncle's hands.

Alice turns toward me and asks, "Auntie, why don't you have a baby in your tummy?"

Oriane smirks and says, "I was wondering exactly the same thing, Alice! You'd love a little cousin, wouldn't you?"

Gabriel comes over, holding Léontine by the hand and wiping his forehead after more than an hour playing with the children. He seems happy. He's lost in thought, but he has a broad smile on his face, as if a huge weight has just been lifted.

I wonder if this would be a good time to bring up the possibility of taking his dog back to the Humane Society.

I'm willing to consider having kids, but I can't be the only one making sacrifices . . .

GABRIEL

At first, when Chloé suggested they renew their wedding vows, Gabriel was skeptical. He had never heard of doing such a thing, so it seemed like just another one of his wife's extravagant whims.

"Would we have to go back to the town hall and church?"

"No, no. No big fuss. We would just prepare some things to say to each other. People usually do it to celebrate a big anniversary or when they've made it through something difficult. I thought it would be a good way for us to start over together."

She explained it all in detail, and he finally decided that it would be the perfect occasion to show their friends and family that the whole reality TV mess was behind them. That he and his wife were moving forward. That he had managed to forgive her and make the best of an absurd situation.

Those closest to him often cited his ability to adapt as one of his best qualities. Flexible, accommodating, amenable. He knows that's how people see him. And that's what he's always been, after all. Agreeable, kind, and considerate. "Easygoing," as his fourth-grade teacher had put it. His mother always shook her head, annoyed. "Easygoing, ha! It's true that he never argues with me when I ask him to clean his room. But if he doesn't want to, he knows just how to sweet talk me with his, 'Oh, of course, Mommy, I'll take care of it straightaway!' And then, when my back is turned, he goes and does whatever he wants!"

Chloé did her best to plan an event he'd enjoy, and he was surprised to discover she actually did know something about what he liked and disliked. She suggested a small, intimate ceremony with only close friends and family.

"There's no need to do a big thing. We could have a barbecue in your parents' backyard, for example. Do you think they'd agree to let us do it in a month? I was thinking Sunday, June 8, would be perfect, because the following Monday is a holiday."

He almost passed out from shock when he heard the word "barbecue."

"You mean no passed hors d'oeuvres, no castles, no layer cakes?"

"I had all that when we got married, honey. This will be about getting together with the people we love . . ."

Gabriel accepted, and his parents were delighted with the idea of having everyone over.

"What a wonderful plan! Plus, I just gave your dad a new gas barbecue for his birthday. He's been dying to try out all sorts of recipes, so it's just perfect!" exclaimed his mother.

Chloé called her parents and sister, and they all accepted the invitation, happy to celebrate the fact that the couple really had put everything behind them. She also invited her three colleagues and her old roommates, Arthur and Guillaume.

Gabriel invited both his sisters, despite the fact that he spent little time with them, and Geoffrey, of course. He also asked Chloé if it would be okay for him to invite Marie-Hélène and Laura, whom he'd gotten to know through the grief group. "Whatever makes you happy, honey," whispered Chloé in his ear. There would be about twenty people total—a far cry from the hundred and fifty guests at their wedding.

At night, before they go to bed, Chloé rests her head on Gabriel's bare chest, and together they fantasize about what to do with the money they've won. They both know they're just dreams, but they still enjoy it.

Chloé thinks about exotic trips with white-sand beaches and turquoise waters. Gabriel suggests trekking through Greenland or Iceland, and she quietly nods. After all, with all the money they've got, they can visit the whole world.

She wants to quit her job and likes thinking about all the exciting things she could do: start a personal trainer company, or develop a line of running clothes or bathing suits—outfits that are both comfortable and fashionable. Why not invest in cutting-edge fabrics and the latest technologies—things that will be all the rage for sports enthusiasts in a few years? Gabriel talks about goat farming in the mountains or opening a bed-and-breakfast in the countryside. Chloé only half listens, wondering if her husband is trying to test her by suggesting things that are diametrically opposed to her ideas.

"Are you serious? Can you really see yourself living in a little stone house on top of a mountain, where a helicopter has to bring you groceries in the winter?"

"Totally! And you could swim in the mountain stream nearby," jokes Gabriel. "I'd make you wear floaties so I wouldn't have to worry."

Chloé bursts into laughter and tells her husband good night. They have to get up early for work the next day.

Gabriel closes his eyes, but before drifting off he savors the idea that soon he won't have to dream about being happy anymore. If the show has taught him anything, it's that he has every right to put himself first from time to time. For years he devoted himself to fulfilling all Chloé's desires, but now he's promised himself not to forget what *he* wants. Not anymore.

EMMA

As I push through the glass door, the bell rings to signal my arrival. The tattoo artist comes over, and I notice that her hair is now a dark turquoise. She snaps her gum in a way she must think is sexy, wearing a jaded look on her face, but it's really just vulgar.

"What do you need?"

I don't think she recognizes me. She seems to enjoy drawing on her customers' skin about as much as I enjoy taking pictures of smiling newlyweds.

"You tattooed an eagle on my wrist almost a year ago, maybe you remember?"

The woman, whose face is covered in piercings, waits for me to continue, totally uninterested. I roll up the sleeve of my leather jacket to show her the inside of my wrist. She gives it a quick glance.

"Yeah, and? It's a little late for complaints."

"I'd like to change it. Is that possible?"

"Depends. Like, I can't turn it into a dolphin."

I want to laugh, but given the frown on her face, I gather it wasn't meant as a joke. I rummage through my bag and pull out a wrinkled piece of paper on which I traced the black eagle as the starting point for my changes, to get an idea of the result. The tattoo artist takes it from my hands and studies it for a second as she blows a bubble with her gum.

"Yeah, it's doable. I can even do it freehand; it'll be quick. You'll be out of here in fifteen minutes. I can fit you in before my next appointment. I mean, if you're sure this time," she adds in a slightly condescending tone.

"Don't worry, I'm sure," I say as I take off my jacket.

"Make yourself at home, then," she replies, gesturing toward the back of the shop.

I sit down in the worn black leather chair. She gets out her equipment, chooses her ink, and turns on the electric needle.

"This will hurt a little."

"I'm aware."

Her lips form a faint smile.

"Well then, here we go."

I close my eyes and exhale as slowly as possible.

Last week, while putting away some things that had been sitting in a corner of my studio for too long, I came across the pale-green envelope Gabriel had given me at our last dinner together. The last time we ever saw each other, as it turned out.

I took out the ticket for Tel Aviv. The job offer I'd gotten to work in Gaza was fake, but the Air France ticket was definitely real. All I had to do was pack my bags, take the train to Charles de Gaulle Airport, and get on the plane to Israel. What did I have to lose? More importantly, what did I stand to gain by staying here?

It was an easy decision. I'd packed the bare minimum in my suitcase; I was sure the rest of my stuff would make the next renter very happy. I comforted my mother on the phone for over an hour, listening to her cry as if she'd just found out her daughter was dead. "You do realize it's a war zone over there, Emma!" My father took the phone away from her in the end and told me to take care of myself. "Let us know

how you're doing, okay? Your mother will drive me nuts if you don't."
He was too proud to admit that he was worried too.

Suddenly the needle stops humming and I unclench my jaw.

"It's done. Told you it wouldn't take long," says the turquoise-haired woman as she quickly cleans my skin and looks at me questioningly. "Like it?"

I glance down and nod. "It's perfect."

Now the eagle has a long tail of crimson and ochre feathers. The black bird of prey has become a magnificent phoenix.

I'm ready to begin my new life.

CHAPTER 19
JUNE 2014

CHLOÉ

Adorable little Alice walks slowly down the aisle holding the ring cushion. She's concentrating so hard on not dropping the rings that it looks like she's trying to freeze them into place with her stare.

"Watch where you're going, sweetheart," says Oriane quietly as her daughter walks past. Alice looks up and smiles when she realizes she's almost reached us.

When Gabriel bends down to take the cushion from our niece's hands, he whispers in her ear. "Thank you very much, little miss!" She blushes with pride, then turns around and runs to rejoin her parents.

I'm nervous. I hate speaking in public. I unfold the paper where I've jotted down my speech. I bite my lip, then relax as I meet Gabriel's reassuring gaze.

"When you agreed to marry me just over four years ago, you pledged yourself to me for better or worse . . . Over the past year, I think I've put you through the worst. You thought I was dead and had to try to move forward without me. Then I came back, and you had to learn to trust me all over again. Today I want to tell you that the 'better' part lies ahead. Now we can finally live our dreams together. I love you, Gabriel, and I'm so happy to be your wife."

I carefully take Gabriel's wedding ring off the cushion and slide it onto his finger. I've had the inside of the white-gold band engraved with the symbolic words *"8 juin 2014 – Pour le meilleur."* For better.

Gabriel smiles at me as our friends and family cheer from the mismatched yard chairs Oriane and my parents brought over earlier. I fold up my little piece of paper and hold it tightly in my closed fist; I don't have a pocket to slip it into. I discreetly adjust the off-white empire-waist dress I bought in a little shop in Rennes last weekend.

Gabriel clears his throat. "Chloé." He pauses and looks deep into my eyes. Seconds pass and I wait to hear the rest.

Everyone is waiting to hear the rest.

He turns to our guests, a smile on his face. "Do you know how Chloé and I met? She noticed me one day outside my bank, smoking on the sidewalk between client meetings. She even changed banks just to meet me! Can you believe that?"

Laughter breaks out.

"She showed up at nine one morning and patiently listened to my speech on savings accounts. Then, all of a sudden, she looked right at me and asked me to lunch. She didn't even give me time to answer before rushing headlong out of my office."

The summarized version makes me blush.

"I should have understood then that when Chloé wants something, she'll do anything to get it. That's definitely still true today!" jokes Gabriel. He turns back toward me and tenderly strokes my cheek. "I love you to death, you know."

He takes my ring and slips it onto my finger. I enjoy the feeling of the cold metal on my skin, a feeling I missed so much. My husband takes my face in his hands and kisses me deeply.

When I finally catch my breath, Gabriel's father stands up and yells, "Let's eat, everyone!"

GABRIEL

Gabriel brought white-chocolate-raspberry cookies he made himself to the final group therapy session. Chloé managed to steal two of them while they were cooling, but he put the rest in a big metal box and told her not to touch them. She promised not to with her mouth full. "Cross my heart," she mumbled, accidentally spitting a few crumbs onto the floor.

Edith thanks him and places the box on a table in a corner of the room, along with the other participants' potluck contributions, all awaiting the meal they'll share after this twelfth and final session.

"Making peace with yourself is the last theme we'll be exploring. Let's go around the table so everyone can share. If you had to compare your state of mind today with your state of mind a year ago, what do you think has changed?"

Gisèle, who's sitting to Edith's left and just celebrated her sixty-fourth birthday, gets things started. She's not one of the most talkative people in the group, but since they're going around the table she doesn't have much of a choice.

"When my husband died in late 2012, I pretended I could cope and get on with my life as before. I wanted to be strong for my kids, who were devastated by the loss of their father. I wanted to protect them, take care of them no matter what. But I didn't have anyone to help *me*. Thanks to the discussions we've had here, I've learned that I'm allowed both to feel pain and to let others see that. Now my two sons are there for me too. I still have a ways to go to get past Guy's death, but I know I'm on the path to healing . . . thanks to all of you."

Gisèle blushes. She's not used to sharing her feelings aloud. The other participants clap quietly, and Edith gently squeezes her forearm to signal her compassion while simultaneously nodding for Michel to take his turn.

"A year ago I was overwhelmed by anxiety attacks. Not a day went by without a panic attack, hot flashes, feeling like my heart was going to burst out of my chest . . . You all remember how hard it was for me to stay seated in this room . . . I felt like I was suffocating. I won't say everything's all better now, but I do feel like I've accepted the fact that anyone can die at any time. That there's nothing fair or unfair about it. And that until then, it's important to take advantage of the time we have."

The others nod in agreement. Laura explains that her grief has become acceptable over the past few months, though it's still with her every single day. She tells them about a man she met a few weeks ago and how she lets herself spend time with him occasionally, without knowing whether it will turn into something more or not.

Marie-Hélène admits that the heavy load of guilt she's been carrying around since her son Sacha's death is getting lighter. She knows now that there was nothing she could have done to save her son and realizes that she has to forgive herself if she wants to go on living.

When it's Oscar's turn to share, he chuckles and says the others have already voiced everything he feels. His pain is getting easier to handle, the desire to scream out loud is ebbing little by little, and the guilt is making way for serenity. His grief, though not gone, is now bearable.

Next Edith turns to Gabriel, who's sitting to her right.

"You're the last one, Gabriel. A few months ago you seemed governed by anger. Is that still the case today?"

Gabriel shakes his head. "When Chloé 'died,'" he says, punctuating his words with air quotes, "I thought I'd never get over it. Nothing made sense anymore, everything was bleak. But when she came back, it turned out to be even worse. I felt like I had lost everything, like I'd been betrayed, manipulated, and humiliated. I didn't think we'd ever be able to survive this together. But I was wrong. Over the weeks, she managed to win me over again, to make me want to trust her. She waited patiently for me to come back to her, gave me the time I needed to get some perspective. And she never stopped believing in us. She never gave up. Today I'm not angry anymore. On the contrary, I feel calm, I'm at peace. As she said when we renewed our vows, the 'better' part lies ahead . . ."

"I think that's a wonderful way to conclude this group's last meeting," says Edith.

"Yes, and it's high time you all tasted my famous cookies!" adds Gabriel with a laugh.

EMMA

"Boarding will begin at terminal 2E, gate 28, in about thirty minutes," explains the woman at check-in as she hands Emma's passport back. Emma watches her red suitcase make its way down the conveyor belt. She takes advantage of the wait to stop by the restroom and then to buy a pack of spearmint gum—she hates having clogged ears on the plane.

"Air France invites all passengers on flight AF354 to Tel Aviv to make their way to gate 28 for immediate boarding."

An airline employee checks her ticket and passport one last time before letting her onto the plane. She takes a copy of *Libération* on her way to her window seat. She distractedly puts her headphones in her ears and starts reading as the other passengers noisily fill the plane.

She doesn't have any idea what she'll do when she gets to Tel Aviv. Strangely, that doesn't worry her at all. On the contrary, actually. She feels light and carefree. She's not even panicking about barely having any money to live on. She feels confident in the future and her talents. With her camera around her neck, she's going to take her chances and see what happens. And if that doesn't work, she can always return home to her parents in Arles. That idea is scary enough to motivate her to do anything and everything necessary to get good photos and sell them to a news agency.

Nathan loaned her two thousand euros before she left. Emma was embarrassed to be asking her little brother for money, when he'd barely been working for two years, but he brushed away her reservations with a shrug.

"I don't see it as a loan, Emma. It's an investment that'll pay dividends very soon. I'll give you two thousand euros, and in exchange, when you get famous, you'll give me an exclusive interview. I can already see my headline, 'Emma Lenglet: Risking Her Life for the Perfect Shot.'"

For now Nathan freelances for a local daily, but he plans to move to Paris someday and work for a national paper.

"Either way I'll pay you back as soon as I can. I don't like having debts."

"Fine, whenever, I'm not worried. But do send me e-mails and let me know where you are, okay? And use some of my money to buy a bulletproof vest!"

Her brother's tone was light, but they both knew the suggestion was hardly a joke.

Emma is pulled from her thoughts by a man trying desperately to fit an oversized bag into the overhead compartment right above her. After squashing it as much as possible, he finally shoves it in, then quickly clicks the latch shut. He sits down in the seat next to Emma and lets out a long sigh.

"I really didn't think it was going to fit! And the flight attendant doesn't seem like the warm and fuzzy type . . . It was a close call!"

He points at one of the women in a navy-blue uniform. Emma has to admit that with her arms crossed behind her back and a rugby player's build, the woman does look pretty menacing. Not the kind who enjoys a good joke.

"Let me tell you a secret . . . Her name is actually Natasha Petroskova. She works for the Russian mob."

"Oh really? What is the Russian mob doing on a flight from Paris to Tel Aviv?" Emma asks skeptically.

"You haven't heard?" he asks dryly. "Their spies are on the lookout for counterfeit vodka! Apparently, they have orders to taste every bottle of water to make sure it's not smuggled booze!"

"That's ridiculous!"

Emma can't help but laugh at his terrible made-up story.

"I'm Benjamin. But everyone calls me Ben."

The man holds out his hand. He looks about Emma's age, maybe a few years older. Short light-brown hair and cheerful green eyes behind lenses in black plastic frames. He has a scar running through one eyebrow and a five-o'clock shadow.

"I'm Emma. But everyone calls me Emma," she mocks.

"Hmm . . . Seems like your sense of humor's about as refined as mine," he answers with a smile.

She shakes his hand.

"So, are you on vacation?" he asks.

Emma is relaxed as they start talking. The flight's about five hours long, so they'll have plenty of time to get to know one another. She tells him that she's a photographer.

"Cool! A kindred spirit. I work for a TV network, and they're always sending me to report from conflict zones. I head out with my video camera and my mic and stay alive however I can. I'm kidding about that last part, but I have made it through a few scrapes."

They talk for a few hours, then Emma goes back to reading her newspaper before dozing off. Her excitement kept her awake last night, so she's catching up on sleep.

Next to her, Benjamin takes off his glasses and discreetly checks that the micro SD card hidden in one of the temples is working. Given everything he had to do to get on the show as a contestant, there's no way he's going to mess everything up now.

CHAPTER 20
JULY 2014

CHLOÉ

Last night Gabriel checked the weather forecast and suggested we have a picnic lunch at our cove today. We haven't been back since I "drowned," and it would be the perfect place to spend some time together and really enjoy each other's company like before.

I'm making chicken sandwiches to put in the plastic cooler while Gabriel gathers some fruit and two bottles of champagne.

"Two bottles, huh? You're trying to get me drunk, aren't you?"

I lean into him and he holds me tight.

"Mrs. Hamon, do you really think I need alcohol to seduce you?"

He bends down to nibble on my ear and I melt instantly. It's crazy how easily he can excite me ever since I came back. It's like I have a new husband, like we just met. The way he takes the initiative now really turns me on. I always used to like to run the show, so I'm pleasantly surprised to see Gabriel in this new light.

We get comfortable on the small beach, still shaded at this time of day. I'd forgotten how calming the sound of the gently crashing waves could be.

Gabriel hands me a glass of champagne.

"To us?"

"To us."

I take a sip and sigh with pleasure. There's nowhere else I'd rather be.

We eat in silence; we don't have to talk to be happy. We simply enjoy the peace and quiet. As we drink glass after glass, Gabriel's hands begin to wander, and I languorously give in to his advances. My head is spinning a bit, and I giggle as he undoes my bra. He kisses my shoulder, my breasts, my stomach. I surrender and enjoy it. After a few minutes, he lies down next to me as I try to catch my breath. I'm too weak to sit up. Gabriel props himself up on his elbow.

"Are you okay?" he asks in a worried tone.

"I'm fine. I'm just . . . a little tipsy!"

I'm feeling so good and carefree, I can't help but laugh. Gabriel's always worrying about me instead of simply sitting back and enjoying the moment.

He leans over me and gently strokes my hair, an affectionate look in his eyes.

"Rest a little, okay? I think we went a bit overboard with the champagne," he says, pointing to the two empty bottles.

"Mmm."

"I'm going to swim a few laps while you take a nap. When you feel better, we'll go home."

My husband gets up and heads toward the water.

"No, wait for me! I want to go swimming too!"

I stagger as I stand up, and Gabriel runs over to catch me.

"That's not a good idea, honey. You're in no state to go swimming right now."

"Oh, come on, Gabriel, don't be such a stick-in-the-mud! It's not like I'm about to pass out! How about you carry me? We could do all sorts of things together in the water . . ."

I'm not sure my suggestion is clear to him. Everything around me is out of focus. I try to concentrate on my husband's hesitant face.

"Come on, carry me!"

Gabriel gives in and carries me into the water.

"Don't let go, okay, Chloé? We won't stay in long . . ."

We wade deeper into the water, his arms tight around me. I close my eyes and let the sun warm my face. Gabriel walks farther out into the waves until the water's up to his chest. He stops and twirls me around gently. Only my head's still dry, and the cool water feels good.

"Stop, Gabriel, I think I'm going to throw up . . ."

GABRIEL

He gazes down at Chloé reassuringly.

"Do you want to go back to the beach?"

"Yes, please. You were right, it wasn't a good idea."

"I'm sorry, what was that?"

"I said you were right. It wasn't a good idea . . ." Chloé mumbles as she runs her hand over her face. She's heavy, floppy, like dead weight in Gabriel's arms.

"What wasn't a good idea? The show?"

Chloé frowns. She can barely open her eyes.

"Huh? What are you talking about? Take me back. I want to go home . . ."

Gabriel takes another step out and Chloé's head goes under. She tries to sit up, clutching at him, but she's too weak. Her arms must weigh a ton, and her brain is clearly moving in slow motion.

"Come on, honey, let's get out . . . I really don't feel well. Apparently I can't handle my champagne . . ."

"Or maybe it's the three Xanax tablets you had with it?"

Chloé manages to open her eyes. She doesn't seem to understand what Gabriel's saying.

"What's it like to be back at the scene of your death?"

"What are you talking about? This isn't funny. I really don't feel well . . . and I'm starting to get cold."

"It's not *funny*?"

Gabriel's voice is thick with irony.

"How *funny* was everything you put me through, huh?"

"We've already talked about all this. We've put it behind us . . ."

Chloé's voice is heavy and she's slurring her words.

Gabriel looks at his wife and decides she doesn't deserve an explanation. Besides, she's probably beyond the point where she could understand anyway. Might as well save his breath.

He wishes she could understand how she destroyed him, how much he's hated her since she came back into his life. For years, he adored her—in every sense of the word. He put her on a pedestal and idolized her. She was the perfect wife and they were the perfect couple. He loved her so much he would have done anything for her, even sacrifice his own needs and desires—and follow her to the ends of the earth. He thought their feelings were reciprocal, thought she loved him just as passionately.

He hadn't been able to love her since the end of that fucking show, but he couldn't just let her leave either. She would have forgotten him all too quickly—especially with all that money. She had to pay for the eight years he had wasted believing in them, in her. Eight years he had spent with a stranger.

He did try to forgive her, but it was no use. Now he feels compelled to see the grieving period he began when she disappeared through to the end. He can't shake the bitter taste in his mouth. The hate has been growing ever since she came back, every time she opens her mouth, every time she laughs. The only thing he ever feels besides hate is disgust. The idea of touching her, of brushing up against her revolts him. But he's hidden it from her and everyone else. He's played the loving, forgiving husband to a T.

Chloé spits and coughs faintly, trying to catch her breath despite the water filling her nose and throat. Gabriel can feel her grasping at him, but she's too weak, her muscles aren't responding.

He's going to drown her nice and slowly. She'll barely resist. It's almost too easy. He would have preferred a real fight, but he knows he can't leave any traces of a struggle on his wife's body if he wants the authorities to deem it an accidental drowning. So he crushed up some antianxiety meds and discreetly mixed them into the champagne, then got her drunk so she wouldn't notice a thing. She never even takes Tylenol, so the alcohol-downer cocktail was even more effective than he'd hoped.

If they ever find the body, the autopsy will reveal that Chloé had taken Xanax and gotten drunk. Gabriel will tell them through his sobs that he'd noticed his wife hadn't been doing well since the show ended, that she'd seemed depressed. She'd been having a hard time getting back into the swing of real life after being cut off from the world for months. She'd been drinking too much, and Gabriel had found several boxes of antidepressants and antianxiety medications in her nightstand. With tears in his eyes, he'll say, "I didn't realize how bad it was. She always put on a strong face; I didn't realize she was struggling." Everyone would believe him, especially since reality TV contestants addicted to alcohol and drugs are a dime a dozen. "My wife is television's latest victim," he'll stutter as he crumples onto the floor. "I'll spend the rest of my life wondering whether it was suicide or an accident . . ."

Everyone will feel sorry for him, the poor man who's been faced with every misfortune. He'll give the five hundred thousand euros to a charity. He doesn't care about the stupid money. And more importantly, he doesn't want anyone to think that he killed his wife to get it all to himself. He'll become a hero instead by giving it away. Yes, he'll give it all to a lifeguard training program or something like that. Perfect. "So no one else will ever drown again!" He can already see himself gazing into the distance, a sorrowful expression in his eyes, chin trembling, inspiring crowds with his speech.

Chloé can't breathe and is starting to gurgle and choke as the water laps into her mouth. The noise pulls Gabriel out of his daydream. He looks at her disapprovingly. Her eyes are like two giant question marks. She doesn't understand why he's doing this. She doesn't understand what's happening to her.

"Shh, shh . . . it'll all be over soon," Gabriel reassures her. "Don't worry, I'll stay with you to the end. I won't leave you."

Chloé tries to push him away but he holds her tightly. She can't fight, she can't escape. She tries to scream but can't manage to make even the slightest sound. A small flock of seagulls flies overhead, and Gabriel is almost sure they're laughing among themselves.

"They'll find you tomorrow, the next day, or a month from now . . . Maybe never. I'll mourn you publicly. I know exactly what it's like to be devastated by my wife's death. After all, I've lived it, remember?"

Chloé closes her eyes for several long seconds. She's giving up. Water covers her face. She opens her mouth over and over, like a fish, instinctively. She's desperately seeking air but keeps swallowing water. Her eyes stare at Gabriel again. *Why why why.*

Her arms relax, then go limp. Her eyes go blank. Gabriel loosens his grip and lets Chloé sink down into the water.

Thank goodness that's over with. Now he can go home and walk Lucky. The poor dog's been locked in the house all day and must be dying to go out.

"Not that you lied to me, but that I no longer believe you, has shaken me."

Friedrich Nietzsche

ACKNOWLEDGMENTS

My first inclination was not to include any acknowledgments, because I was afraid of forgetting or hurting someone important.

But as time passed, I realized that I would regret not paying tribute to all the people who had helped turn the life of this independent author into a waking dream.

First and foremost, I would like to thank Mathieu, who puts up with me all day every day, providing steadfast support, and who has stood by my side since the very beginning of this adventure.

I would also like to acknowledge:

My father, who was one of this novel's earliest defenders. He was always forthcoming with advice, ready to read and reread successive versions on the hunt for the tiniest discrepancy or typo.

My sister, who now prefaces her confidences with, "This won't end up in one of your books, will it?"

Mélanie, for her sincere enthusiasm and unfailing encouragement.

Frédéric, whose trained eye was an incredible help in reworking the text at a moment when I had lost perspective on the story I had imagined.

Claire, for rekindling the somewhat crazy idea that I should write a novel.

I would also like to express my heartfelt thanks to the wonderful community of independent authors I am honored to be a part of. In particular, I am indebted to Patrick Ferrer, Jacques Vandroux, and Alice Quinn for their precious advice.

And I could never forget Solène Bakowski. The seagulls are for you!

I of course owe a huge thank-you to the thousands of readers who have talked about, blogged about, and reviewed the original French version of *Interference* since I published it in March 2015. Some of them even took the time to write directly to me.

Special thanks go out to Julien Arnaud, my first "unknown" reader.

I wish to express my appreciation to the Amazon France and US teams for their support, creativity, and ambition to share *Interference* with as many readers as possible.

Many thanks to Florian Lafani at Editions Michel Lafon, who probably had no idea how hard my heart was pounding during our first phone call . . .

I would also like to acknowledge my English translator, Maren Baudet-Lackner, for her work approximating my style and faithfully conveying the voices of my characters.

Last but not least, my thanks go out to you, of course, you who dared buy my first novel, who bet on me—a nobody. My fingers are crossed that I haven't disappointed you.

If, by any chance, you started reading *Interference* before going to bed, I hope I managed to keep you up all night!

ABOUT THE AUTHOR

Photo © 2012

Amélie Antoine lives in northern France with her husband and two children. She has always loved writing, particularly stories. In 2011, she published an autobiography titled *Combien de Temps*. *Interference* is her first novel and was an immediate success when it was released in France, winning the *Première Lauréate du Prix Amazon de l'Auto-Édition* (Amazon France Self-Publishing Prize) for best self-published e-book. She has since written two other novels.

ABOUT THE TRANSLATOR

Photo © 2015 Flora Chevalier

Maren Baudet-Lackner grew up in New Mexico. After earning a BA from Tulane University in New Orleans, a Master's in French Literature from the Sorbonne, and an M.Phil. in the same subject from Yale, she moved to Paris, where she now lives with her husband and children. She has translated several works from the French, including the contemporary thriller *It's Never Too Late* by Chris Constantini and the nineteenth-century memoir *The Chronicles of the Forest of Sauvagnac* by the Count of Saint-Aulaire.